the Fear Zone

the Fear Zone

K. R. Alexander

Scholastic Inc.

Copyright © 2019 by Alex R. Kahler writing as K. R. Alexander

All rights reserved. Published by Scholastic Inc., *Publishers since 1920.* SCHOLASTIC and associated logos are trademarks and/or registered trademarks of Scholastic Inc.

ISBN 978-1-338-57717-4

10 9 8 7 6 5 4 3 2 1   19 20 21 22 23

Printed in the U.S.A.   40
First printing 2019

Book design by Baily Crawford

For those brave enough
to face their fears

PART ONE
the dare

April

"Hey, give that back!" I yelp.

Andres grins, which looks really creepy since he's wearing fake vampire fangs for Halloween. He doesn't hand back the folded piece of orange paper he's snatched from my locker—instead he takes a step back and waves it while other costumed kids walk down the hall around us. He's been my best friend since sixth grade, and even now, two years later, he sometimes acts like my little brother. My very annoying little brother.

Andres starts opening the folded letter.

"Come on, give it back."

Andres shakes his head, still smiling, unfolding the note slowly.

Honestly, I have no idea what the note is, and I don't want Andres to be the first to find out. Maybe it's from a friend telling me about a last-minute Halloween party. Or maybe it's from my archnemesis, Caroline, telling me I look ugly in my black cat costume. It wouldn't surprise me. She's gone from good friend to enemy ever since last year.

I feebly snatch at the paper one more time, but Andres dances back a step. The page is almost entirely unfolded now.

He reads it to himself. His smile slips.

"What is this?" he asks. "Some sort of joke?"

He turns the paper over, and I read what's written in messy paint on the other side.

MEET IN THE GRAVEYARD.
TONIGHT. MIDNIGHT.
OR ELSE.

"Huh?" I ask. I grab for the paper again. This time he lets me have it. "Who wrote this?"

Andres shrugs and leans against the locker beside mine.

"Maybe it's a prank?" he says.

I keep rereading the note. I don't recognize the handwriting. It's not Caroline's, that's for sure. I don't think I have any other enemies at Jackson Middle School.

Do I?

I want to crumple up the letter, but when I look at it again, chills race down my spine. Those two words: *Or else*.

Or else *what*?

"It has to be a prank," I reply. "A Halloween scare. I bet some kids from the high school are going to be there to scare us or something."

It wouldn't surprise me. Kids in our town love Halloween, and I've heard a bunch of stories about high school kids taking the scares too far. Dressing up as monsters and running after little kids. Throwing pumpkins on cars. Apparently, years ago, a kid even went missing while playing hide-and-seek in the graveyard, and wasn't found until the next morning.

I shudder and crumple the note, tossing it in a

nearby trash can. Whatever this is, I don't want any part in it.

"Come on," I say. I shut my locker and zip up my bag. "Let's go. I think Mom finally brought all the Halloween candy out of hiding."

"You had me at *candy*," Andres says. He takes my arm, and together we walk down the hall and out of the school. But no matter how loudly we talk about other things, I'm haunted by the feeling:

Someone wants me to be at the graveyard.

At midnight.

Someone wants me to be afraid.

Andres

We walk down the halls of Jackson Middle School and all I can think about is who left that weird note in her locker. Caroline? I could totally see her doing something like that, but it seems too . . . I don't know, too obvious. Caroline's more the type to spread nasty rumors than leave creepy notes.

I should know.

Ever since last year, Caroline has seen me as an enemy too. Which bites, since Caroline and I used to be friends when we worked in the drama department together.

I can tell April's freaked out—and I don't want to freak her out any more. So I don't tell her that I got a similar note in my locker. Only, my note wasn't as scary. It didn't threaten me. It just said:

MIDNIGHT. GRAVEYARD. PREPARE TO BE SCARED.

Which makes me think this is all some elaborate prank being played on the eighth graders rather than a vengeance thing by Caroline. Either that, or it's some sort of party.

I plan on going either way. If it's Caroline trying to be scary, I *have* to see her fail. And if it's a party, I don't want to miss out.

I do what I can to cheer up April as we walk to her house. Pretty much everyone we pass is in costume. There are the usual zombies and mummies made of toilet paper, the costumes kids put together last minute. Others have clearly put a lot of thought into it. I pass by a pirate with a squawking stuffed bird on his shoulder. I nearly jump back when I see he has a plastic shark eating his leg. A very realistic shark.

Our town goes all out on Halloween night, and this year our trick-or-treat is going to be huge. They've closed down all of the main street downtown and set up stalls with vendors giving away free candy and hot cider, and April's house is right around the corner. We're going to have *tons* of visitors. I can't wait. April no longer seems as enthusiastic.

"We're still on door duty, yeah?" I ask.

She nods. Clearly, she's still thinking about the note.

"Mom is taking Freddy out tonight. It's his first trick-or-treat."

"Cute," I say. "Just means we get to eat all the candy ourselves!"

She smiles, but I can tell her heart isn't in it.

"It's nothing," I say. I nudge her. "Just some kids playing a prank. They probably didn't even know it was your locker. I bet it was random." I have to stop myself from saying, *I bet everyone got one*, because then she'd ask if I got one, and I know that wouldn't end well.

She half smiles at me; it's not convincing.

"Look at that!" I point at a nearby yard. "So cool."

The yard has been completely transformed into a horror scene. There are open caskets with moving skeletons inside and giant cauldrons filled with smoke and green light. Animatronic bats flap around on the front porch, and fabric ghosts hang from the trees, billowing in the breeze.

"Whoa," she says. "They must have spent a bunch of money."

One of the standing caskets opens as we pass.

With a terrifyingly loud giggle, a clown with a giant red smile pops out, his hands raised to grab us.

April yelps and jumps back, nearly knocking me over. I catch her before she tumbles off the sidewalk into traffic.

"It's okay!" I say. "It's fake!"

We pause there for a moment, staring at the mannequin as it angles back into the coffin and the door shuts. April's hand is on her heart and her breath is fast. She stares at the closed casket with wide eyes.

"Why?" she gasps. "Why does it always have to be clowns?"

I squeeze her shoulders. "Because everyone's afraid of clowns. Even clowns are afraid of clowns. It's, like, human nature or something." Even though I know that's not the reason *she's* scared of clowns, I would never bring it up. There are certain things that we don't talk about, and *clowns* are one of them.

"But you aren't scared of them," she says. She doesn't take her eyes off the casket. "You aren't scared of anything."

"Not true," I say. I start walking—there's another group of kids coming up behind us, and I don't want her to be near when the clown springs out again. "I'm terrified of sharks."

"We live in Iowa," she replies. "There's literally no way to be afraid of sharks here. Unless you go to the aquarium or something."

"You tell that to five-year-old me, who refused to take baths for a year because he watched a shark documentary."

April chuckles. Phew. At least she's no longer thinking about the note.

"Scared of a stupid yard decoration, April?" someone calls from behind us.

I grimace before I even look back.

Of course. Caroline.

"Just keep walking," I mutter under my breath.

April doesn't. She stops and turns around, her hands on her hips.

"I wasn't scared," she says. "Just surprised."

"Please," Caroline says. She steps up to us and

sneers. Which is super effective, since she's dressed as a green wicked witch, complete with a long warty nose and black lipstick. She eyes April up and down, and the sneer widens. Oh no. "What are you dressed as, anyway? A scaredy-cat?"

Caroline's two friends—Lia is dressed like an angel, Joann a devil, which seems a little too appropriate—cackle with laughter.

"Good one, Caroline," Angel says. "Scaredy-cat."

"More like scaredy-*fat*," Devil replies. "Look at her."

They all start laughing and point at April's costume. It's a simple costume, but it works—a black T-shirt and jeans, a black tail, ears, and painted whiskers. She was proud of it when we did her makeup this morning. Now she practically deflates.

Fat jokes. How creative.

Anger fills my chest with heat.

"This coming from the girl who finally dressed as her true self," I say, looking between the devil girl and Caroline.

Caroline's laughter cuts short. She glares at me.

"What are you supposed to be, anyway? Aren't vampires supposed to be pale?"

I roll my eyes. Who says vampires can't be Latinx?

"Wow," I say. "Ugly *and* unoriginal. That costume really does suit you. Or is today the day you finally took your costume *off*?"

Caroline says something under her breath that I know is insulting, but I don't hear it. I've already turned and taken April by the arm. Together, we cross the street and continue walking home. Thankfully, Caroline and her goonies don't come after us.

"You didn't have to do that," April says when we're a block away.

"What, defend my best friend?" I shrug. "I'm not going to stand around and listen to ignorant people insult you."

"They're going to come after you now," she says. And maybe I was wrong before. Maybe clowns aren't the things that scare April the most. Maybe it's bullies like Caroline.

"Whatever. I'd like to see them try."

"You wouldn't," she whispers.

I squeeze her arm again. Last year, Caroline went from being one of April's best friends to her worst enemy. It seemed to happen without any warning. We hadn't heard from Caroline all summer break, and when she got back to school, she was just . . . distant. April tried to connect with her, but Caroline lashed out, saying she didn't need friends like April. Since then, Caroline has made it a point to be as mean to April as possible, no matter how much April once tried to be her friend. Sometimes she takes it too far. Lately, it seems like whenever Caroline sees April, she has a new, cruel name thought up for her.

If anything is evil incarnate, it's her.

"Don't worry about me," I say. "Or her. Come on! It's Halloween. Let's go stuff ourselves with candy and dance to terrible pop music."

"I don't think I want any candy," April says.

I sigh.

"We can still dance around like idiots?" I say hopefully.

She smiles—this time, for real.

"Yeah, we can."

I take her arm and do a stupid little dance to make her giggle before we set off toward home.

I feel like I'm being watched.

I turn around, thinking that maybe it's April, staring daggers at my back.

But there's no one there.

Just that clown still popped out of his casket,

reaching.

Deshaun

"Ugh, not those three," I mutter.

Kyle walks beside me, and we eye Caroline and her horrible friends out of the corners of our eyes.

"Just keep walking." Kyle nudges me forward.

I watch the kids who Caroline was picking on cross the street and walk a few feet in front of us. I think they go to the middle school—I remember the girl, April, from band last year, and I recognize her friend but don't know his name. Caroline, though . . . she's pretty much infamous, even in the high school.

"So," Kyle continues. "What's the plan for tonight?

Are you handing out candy or are we going to Sarah's party?"

"Candy duty," I say. "Could maybe try to hit up the party after."

"Do you want company?" he asks.

"You don't have to," I reply. "It's just going to be sitting around in costume for a few hours watching stupid movies."

We'd both much rather be trick-or-treating, but we aren't sure if going door-to-door would be seen as uncool now that we're freshmen. And seeing as Sarah is one of the most popular kids in our grade, her party seems like the next best thing. Even though neither of us really wants to go. At least, I don't.

"Let's see," he says, ticking off the options on his fingers. "I could either go to a party where I don't know or even really like anyone, or I could spend the night wearing my awesome costume with you and eating all the candy I want. Choices, choices . . ."

I snort. "Yeah, but . . . I don't know, won't people notice if you aren't there?"

Unlike me, Kyle is actually popular—when we walk through the halls, people high-five him and know his name. It helps that he plays football and is on the swim team. I'm just the band geek.

"I don't care about other people," Kyle says. "I wanna actually enjoy my night."

I grin in spite of myself.

"Well then, pizza and candy and bad scary movies it is."

"Yes," he replies. "And maybe, if we get bored, we can go to the party after."

I know in the back of my mind that it means he actually *does* want to go to the party, and he's just hanging with me to be nice. We've been friends since kindergarten; he knows I don't want to go, and he doesn't want me to be home alone on our favorite holiday. He's a good friend. I feel bad for holding him back. I decide I'll get extra toppings on the pizza and pick his favorite movie, to make up for it.

I might even let him convince me to go to the party after.

Just the thought is enough to make me feel sick to my stomach. Freshman year hasn't been fun—no one seems to care that I exist, and even with Kyle around I still feel alone. A small part of me thinks that maybe if I show up to the party tonight, that will all change.

People will see me in my cool costume and I'll magically say cool things and then suddenly I'll be cool. Like Kyle. The majority of me knows that will never be the case. But still. I'll go. If it makes him feel better.

Maybe.

We head inside and throw our stuff in my room. My room is a disaster area right now—clothes in piles in every corner, my guitar thrown on top of my unmade bed, and pages of old homework scattered along the floor like leaves. Anyone else, and I would feel self-conscious about inviting them in. But this is Kyle. He practically lives here. Honestly, half of the time, he does. He even has his own drawers in my closet and the bathroom.

He tosses his backpack against the wall and settles into the beanbag by my TV, nudging some controllers out of the way.

"What you going to dress up as?" he asks.

I look to my closet. Half of it is filled with costumes from when we go to cons. Everything from Renaissance attire to full-on mech-gear anime. Much of it he's helped make, because I am terrible at sewing and picking out clothes.

"Dunno," I say. "Depends on if we're going out, I guess. When is it, anyway?"

Because if I'm staying inside, I'm putting on a unicorn onesie. If we're going out, I might put in a bit more effort. I think there's a really creepy alien outfit I could wear, hiding in the back. We had considered going to school in costume, but we weren't certain if anyone else was. We didn't want to look like fools. It seemed like everyone had had the same worry—only about half of the kids were in costume, and they'd been lackluster at best. Clearly, there was a big difference between high school and middle school.

"Let me check," Kyle says.

He rummages in his bag, and in doing so, he knocks over my own bag. Papers and books spill out, but one piece of paper catches both of our attention. It's orange and crumpled into a tight ball.

"What's that?" I ask. I don't remember that being in there. "Is that the invite?"

I can't imagine anyone would sneak a party invite into my bag, but that's the only explanation I can come up with. I know it wasn't there when I was putting in my homework.

He unfolds it. His eyebrow rises as he hands it over to me.

MEET IN THE GRAVEYARD.
TONIGHT. MIDNIGHT.
OR ELSE.

"That's a really creepy party invite," I say. Inside, I cringe. The graveyard is the absolute last place I ever want to go again.

"This isn't the invite. At least, not the one I got. This one sounds really scary." His eyes honestly light up with excitement. "We should go."

April

Andres is passed out on the sofa by nine.

Mom and Freddy have already returned from trick-or-treating, and we got to laugh our butts off watching a very hyper four-year-old run around in a T. rex onesie while Mom chased him down, saying he needed to change for bed. It was Andres who managed to corral Freddy into his bedroom by pretending to be a velociraptor, and even then, Freddy only agreed to go to bed when Mom said he could sleep in his costume.

Credits are rolling for the third cheesy horror movie we watched and a plastic cauldron of half-eaten candy sits between us. It's Friday night, and

Mom has already said Andres can sleep here. Honestly, he sleeps over here most weekends anyway, often passing out on the bottom futon of Freddy's bunk bed.

I glance over at Andres. His fangs are out and the fake blood is smeared all over his chin and the eyeliner we gave him is smudged so he looks sort of like a goth rock star. Well, except for the drool dribbling down his lip. I snicker.

"Hwa?" he asks, pushing himself up straight as he tries to wake up. "I wasn't sleeping."

"Right, right," I say. "Who was the killer, then?"

"A pumpkin," he replies drowsily. His eyes are already shut and he's sinking back into the sofa. I doubt he'll even make it up to Freddy's room at this rate.

Sugar crashes are real.

He easily ate a whole bag of candy. Good thing he runs track, or else he'd get . . .

I force myself not to go down that train of thought. It's Halloween. I'm not going to let anything ruin my favorite holiday. Especially not my cruel inner thoughts. As Andres always tells me—Caroline is enough of a bully on her own. She doesn't need me to help her make my life miserable.

"Come on," I say. I toss a piece of candy at him. "It's bedtime."

"Not tired," he mumbles. He doesn't budge.

I start laughing.

"Dude, you're already asleep."

I don't know if it's my laughter or the next five pieces of candy I toss at him, but he finally wakes up with a huge yawn.

"You're wasting candy," he says.

"Oh please, you'll eat it."

He smiles and, in response, opens one of the candies in his lap and pops it into his mouth.

"Uck, I don't know how you can keep eating sugar," I groan. "I swear I just want, like, kale for the next week."

"Years of training," he replies. "And I quickly learned that the only way to hide candy from my brothers was to eat it."

He snatches another piece of candy as if demonstrating his point, but stops halfway through unwrapping it. His eyes are wide and locked on the TV.

"Hey," he says. "Is that part of the movie?"

I glance at the TV to see what he's talking about and nearly yelp in fear.

The credits have ended, but rather than going back to the site's homepage, there's a single line of text on the screen.

YOU HAVE THREE HOURS

"What the heck?" I ask. Chills race down my spine and it takes all my self-control not to run over and push the TV off its stand.

"Maybe it's some sort of . . ." Andres trails off, because he clearly can't come up with a rational explanation either.

"Maybe that's, like, how much longer it's available to stream?" I ask.

Andres jolts upright.

"The cemetery."

"What?"

"The cemetery," he says. "The note in your locker. It said we were supposed to meet there at midnight, right? That's in three hours."

After Caroline's taunting and a few hours of bad movies and sugar, I'd forgotten all about the note I'd trashed. Now that he's reminded me, I can't help but feel like we're being watched. I glance out the window and see only darkness. It doesn't make me feel any better.

Andres is standing now, and he actually seems excited.

I want to sink into the sofa and under all the blankets and never come out again.

"We aren't going anywhere," I say. "Definitely not to a graveyard. This is probably, just, I don't know . . ."

"Oh, come on, April. Where's your sense of adventure?"

This is the big difference between Andres and me. He sees things as adventures. I see them as dangers.

"Adventure?" asks my mom, stepping into the living room. "Who's going adventuring at this hour?"

She's changed out of her costume—she'd gone as a paleontologist, complete with a khaki hat and notebook and everything—and into pajamas. She's also holding a giant mug of tea.

"It's nothing," I say. "Andres was just trying to talk me into another scary movie."

Mom glances at the television and my heart flips

over itself. But the moment she looks to the TV, the words are gone. What in the world?

"It's already late," Mom says. "And I'm pretty certain I heard Andres snoring earlier."

"I don't snore!" he protests.

He totally snores.

"And besides," he continues, "I've just had more candy. It's my second wind!"

Mom chuckles. "Well, normally I'd say you need to get to sleep, but I know it's your favorite holiday and it's a weekend." She smiles. "So, one more. Then you need to get to bed."

Her smile turns into a yawn.

"I'm going to go read and pass out. I'm trusting you two to go to sleep once the movie's over, okay? Try not to scare yourselves too badly. I don't want April having to sleep in my room again."

"That was only one time three years ago and it was a very scary movie about clowns!" I say. I feel the heat rush to my cheeks. Not that the story is a surprise to Andres—he was there. It was one of the first nights he'd stayed over. I'd let him convince me to watch a terrifying movie about clowns from space. I got so scared that I had to sleep in Mom's bed. Ever since that birthday party . . .

He'd laughed, but he didn't rub it in. He also never brought it up again, which is how I knew he was going to be a good friend. After that, the only horror movies we watched were B-grade eighties flicks. No clowns. No sharks.

Mom gives us each a hug and then heads back upstairs. We listen for her footsteps to recede, and then Andres looks at me. His face once more shines with excitement.

"So?" he asks.

"So?"

"Are we going to do it?"

I look back to the TV. The words are still gone, and it starts to make me wonder if we made it up. Some sugar-induced hallucination or something.

"I don't know . . ."

"Pleeeeeease."

"The note didn't say anything about you going," I say. "And it didn't sound like it was going to be a fun time. I mean, that whole *or else* part seemed ominous. What if you got hurt?"

"We'll bring a baseball bat if you're that worried, and we have phones if there's any real trouble. It's fine. Besides, we don't have to actually go *into* the graveyard. We can just hang out in the bushes and watch to see who's there. It's just going to be some kids from school pulling a stupid Halloween prank. I want to watch them try."

"How do you explain that, then?" I ask, pointing at the blank TV. I grab the remote and rewind it a few frames. There's nothing on there. No creepy text. No nothing. Just the normal credits and blackness.

Andres shrugs. "Maybe someone hacked in? I don't know. I just know we can't miss out on this."

I don't know why Andres is so enthusiastic about going or how he can pass this off as normal. Probably because he isn't the one getting creepy notes in his locker or messages on his TV. Or maybe it's because— unlike me—he enjoys being scared.

I also know that if we *don't* go tonight, I'll never hear the end of it. And I can just imagine school on Monday—all the kids talking about the party or prank or whatever that we missed out on because I was too scared.

If Caroline's behind it, I refuse to give her the satisfaction of me chickening out.

"Okay," I finally agree. "But if we're going, we *aren't* watching a scary movie beforehand."

Andres's smile widens.

"Deal."

Kyle

We leave Deshaun's house at a quarter to midnight.

He didn't really have to try to convince me to skip the party. Even though I was hoping to go and meet some new people, I could tell he was bummed over not getting an invite. And I think the creepy note thing scared him more than he wanted to let on. He kept bringing it up all through the cheesy horror movies we watched, how he was wondering if this meant someone was watching or following him. I knew what he was really scared of, though: He was worried this meant he was going to be pranked, which meant he was still a nerd, just like we had been in middle school.

He'd hoped that going to high school would change everything for him. Trouble was, it hadn't.

Which is also why neither of us is in costume. We're both wearing black, and I have some creepy animal masks in my backpack just in case this *does* end up being a costume party. Gotta leave our options open.

"Do we really have to do this?" Deshaun whispers. I've never heard him so scared before—why is he so freaked out about a couple high schoolers throwing a prank?

We creep along the sidewalk outside his house. Everyone inside is asleep, and the last thing we need is for his mom to wake up and find us sneaking out.

"Yes," I say. "We're in high school now. We have to face our problems head-on."

It's something my dad has said more times than I want to admit.

And by *said*, I mean *yelled*.

I push down thoughts of him—he's not going to ruin tonight.

"Besides," I continue, patting Deshaun on the shoulder, "you *know* this is just some seniors pranking underclassmen. I wanna see what they're up to—I can guarantee you it's not nearly as scary as the things we've dreamed up."

For a few years, we set up a mini haunted house in Deshaun's basement and invited our friends over to check it out. It wasn't exactly the scariest thing in the world, but I know it was innovative, and I know whatever the graveyard prank tonight is, it won't be nearly as cool as what Deshaun and I created.

Deshaun mutters something under his breath.

"I'm just going to pretend that's you thanking me for having your back," I say.

"If you had my back, we would still be in pajamas eating candy," he replies. He shivers. "Where it's warm."

I chuckle and keep walking.

The night feels colder than normal, and a thin fog twists over the ground. We pass by darkened houses and front lawns filled with Halloween decorations. A chill creeps over me as we walk—the decorations look even more ghostly in the dead of night. Giant scarecrows tower over us ominously, sheet ghosts sway in the cold breeze, hanging from gnarled trees that look like witches' fingers. A few pumpkins glow on porches, their candlelight flickering from jeering faces like lost souls. The light casts strange shadows over the yards, long and sharp like talons or spirits. It makes my skin crawl, but that just makes me more excited. I love being scared.

"So. Creepy," I whisper.

Deshaun just shudders.

We trek through the neighborhood and toward the cemetery at the edge of town. Thankfully, Mapleville isn't a very big place, and the graveyard is only a few blocks away. Every step we take, I swear the air gets colder. It's so quiet I can hear the blood pounding in my ears and every one of our quiet footsteps. Except for when the wind blows; then the world is filled with hissing. It reminds me way too much of the snakes Dad keeps in the basement.

Just the thought makes my skin crawl. A dark basement of snakes is *not* what I need to be thinking about right now.

I'd never admit it out loud, but I'm starting to wonder if this was a bad idea. If this is a party in the graveyard, why can't we hear music when we're only a block away?

Deshaun stops suddenly.

"Wait," he whispers. "Do you hear that?"

I strain my ears, but I don't hear anything. Until . . .

"Footsteps!" I hiss. We crouch and glance around. Streetlamps illuminate the sidewalk, and there isn't really anywhere good to hide unless we run into someone's yard, and they might have dogs and—

"Who's there?" someone calls softly.

"April?" Deshaun replies.

Shadows turn into people, and sure enough, the girl and her friend we saw earlier step out into the street.

"Deshaun? What are you doing here?" April asks. "Did you get a note too?"

Deshaun swallows hard. "Yeah," he says. "You?"

Both April and her friend nod. He's cute and familiar, but I don't know his name.

"I'm Kyle," I say, holding out my hand.

"Andres," the guy replies. His handshake is firm, and he smiles as he takes my hand. "This is my friend April," he says.

I take her hand and shake it too.

"So you each got a note?" I ask.

"Just me," April says.

"Actually," Andres interrupts with a gulp, "I got

one too." He glances at April, who looks shocked by his admission. "Sorry. Didn't want to freak you out."

"Consider me freaked," April says. She turns back to us. "Did both of you get the note?" she asks.

I shake my head no. "Just along for the ride."

"He forced me to go," Deshaun says glumly.

"Andres did too."

"Come on," I reply. "We're already out here. Might as well see it through, right?"

We all look toward the end of the road, to where the graveyard waits. A cold wind slithers around us, rustling leaves and making the hanging ghosts in nearby yards come alive.

"That doesn't seem ominous at all," April mumbles.

"Come on," I repeat. "There's four of us. What's the worst that could happen?"

"I wish you hadn't said that," Deshaun says.

We walk.

April

I don't know what I expect when we creep up to the graveyard. A party? A bunch of skeletons or demons roaming around? Instead, the field of tombstones is empty. A heavy moon hangs in the sky, clouds thick and glowing silver, just enough to cast light over the rows and rows of squat stone and stunted trees. Maybe there are kids hiding somewhere amid the tombstones. Maybe no one is here at all, and this was just a prank to get us out of our houses, to see who is the most gullible.

I'd thought this was all a prank from Caroline, but the fact that Deshaun and his friend Kyle are here makes me think this is bigger than her. Unless she has some vendetta against them that I don't know about. I can't imagine why, though. Deshaun and I were in band together last year, and he always seemed nice enough. He was really good at trumpet too. Nothing that would put a target on his back.

The four of us trek silently into the graveyard, our phones out as flashlights. Andres hadn't lied—he brought a baseball bat, and he holds it at his side now, just barely dragging it on the grass. Even that small sound seems louder than thunder out here. I swear that none of us even breathe.

We walk past the iron gate that's always open, up a low hill covered in mounds and stones, past twisted trees. The air is so cold I'm shivering, and the constant wind doesn't help. Every gust rustles the leaves, makes tree limbs scratch against each other. I'm suddenly reminded of the zombie flick we watched before coming here. The screen had looked exactly like this . . .

The sound of laughter makes me stop dead in my tracks.

I look around at the shadows surrounding us, the tombstones hiding sneering skulls and monsters. It wasn't a little girl's laughter. No, it was male. It sounded like . . .

"Did you hear that?" I ask, straining my ears.

"Hear what?" Deshaun asks.

"That laughter." I swallow loudly. "It sounded like a clown."

The moment I say it, more chills shudder across my skin. That high-pitched, diabolical laugh seemed to come from everywhere at once, and suddenly I am back at my birthday party, back in front of the crowd of kids, back beside the clown while he laughs and points, along with everyone I thought was my friend. I immediately push the memory away and force down the tears that are starting to rise.

Hearing the laughter is one thing, but admitting out loud that I heard it is another. It makes the sound real. It makes me think that there is a clown out there, waiting for me to turn my back, waiting to jump out and scream and torment me.

I don't want to move another step. At least, I don't want to move another step if it isn't back toward the safety and warmth of my home.

Andres seems to notice. He squeezes my hand and inches in a little closer.

"I want to go," I say, barely above a whisper.

Andres doesn't say anything. Just squeezes my

hand again and looks at the boys who've joined us. I know they won't listen to me, but maybe Andres will.

"Maybe she's right," Andres says.

"About the laughter?" Kyle asks. "I didn't hear anything. Did you?"

Both Deshaun and Andres shake their heads, but Deshaun looks uncertain about it.

"I meant maybe she's right—we should go," Andres continues. He looks at Kyle as he says it, as it's clear Kyle is the only one who actually wants to be out here. "I mean, look—there isn't anyone out. No party, no upperclassmen. We're just alone in an empty graveyard at midnight and it's cold and who knows what sort of creepers might be out here. This was just a prank, and not a very good one. I say we call it a night and go. Before the cops come or our parents realize we're gone. I don't want to be grounded."

It's nice of him to mention that, since his own parents think he's at my house, and wouldn't ground him even if they knew. He's saying all of this for my sake. And it seems to be working.

"Maybe you're right," Deshaun says. "Come on, Kyle. There's nothing out here and I'm getting cold. I'd rather be at that stupid party than out here."

Kyle seems to be ready to admit defeat as well. Then something catches his eye.

"Look!" he says, pointing. "Over there!"

On the next small hill is a flickering golden light, like a candle in the dark.

"That must be it," Kyle says excitedly.

Deshaun doesn't look like he wants to go over there. Neither do I.

"Come on," Andres says. He takes my hand reassuringly; his palm is warm, and it roots me down, helps me keep away some of my fear. My best friend is here. Nothing bad can happen.

If only I actually believed this.

We trek over to the candle, our feet crunching way too loudly on leaves and branches, and it's only when we reach the light that I realize it's coming from a pumpkin. Its face is carved with jagged teeth and fierce eyes, and even though I've seen literally hundreds of carved pumpkins, this one seems . . . worse. Alive. Like the flame behind its eyes is breathing an evil life into it, like it's watching our every move.

It sits atop an old tombstone. There aren't any names engraved in the surface—it's been worn smooth by rain and wind and time. But someone has recently come and vandalized it.

Carved in the stone are the words:

DO NOT DISTURB

Then, spray-painted on top in red, in the exact same handwriting as my note, are two words:

FIND ME

and an arrow pointing toward the freshly churned dirt at its base.

Something has been buried here. And I know in the darkest pit of my gut that we are supposed to dig it up.

"Okay, guys," I say. I look around; the four of us all stand silently around the grave, none of us moving or making a sound. It's so cold now that goose bumps cover all of my skin, and so quiet I can hear Andres's breath at my side. His hand still holds mine, but even though his hand is warm, it's starting to shake. "We came to the graveyard. We saw the creepy note. Can we go home now?"

Because now that we're here, it's clear that no one else is showing up. There isn't a hidden crowd of upperclassmen among the tombstones waiting to jump out and prank us. There isn't a party happening in a nearby mausoleum.

There is just the four of us and this creepy grave and a silence deeper than death and a warning that I desperately want to heed. The last thing I want to do is disturb this grave, and it looks like everyone else is on the same page. Even Kyle's excitement is diminished; he keeps staring at the tombstone, his pale face even paler in the ghostly glow of the candle.

"Yeah," Kyle says. "I think we should go."

"Already?" comes a voice from behind us. "But we haven't even gotten to the good part yet."

I turn my head slowly, but I know who it is before we lock eyes.

Caroline.

Andres

Caroline is literally the last person any of us wants to see, as is made clear by the glares everyone casts her way when she walks up, swinging her flashlight around like this is her party. April's fists are clenched tight at her sides.

"Caroline," April growls. "Is this your doing?"

"Maybe," she says with a smug smile. "Why, are you scared?"

"No," Kyle says. "Just annoyed. Why'd you drag us out here in the dead of night?"

A shiver rolls down my spine at the word *dead*. I've never liked graveyards; all those dead bodies buried only six feet below me. Waiting. Decomposing.

Watching. It makes my skin crawl. I move closer to April and tighten my grip on the bat; it's not Caroline I'm worried about, but all the things I can't see.

Caroline just rolls her eyes at Kyle's accusation. "I didn't, moron. I had nothing to do with this. I just saw you sneaking off and decided to follow you. What are we doing out here, anyway?"

No one says anything, but then she catches sight of the marked tombstone. Her eyes practically light up, glowing as fiercely as the pumpkin's.

"Oooh," she says. Her voice wavers theatrically, like a ghost's. "*So* creepy."

She takes a step closer to the tombstone. In that moment, Kyle steps closer to me. His body practically radiates heat, and I want to lean in. I am so. Cold. And it seems to be getting colder by the minute. The sky is crystal clear, though—no storms anywhere. Maybe that's why it's so chilly out here; there isn't any cloud cover to keep in the heat.

I'm not currently worried about the weather or the chills on my skin or even the way April shakes beside me with anger or cold. My eyes are glued on Caroline. Whether she had something to do with all of this or not, her being here is *not* a good thing. If we make it out of the graveyard without Caroline insulting April, it will be a Halloween miracle. Plus, I don't trust the way she's eyeing the freshly churned grave.

"What do you think is in here?" she asks. She kneels down and runs her hands over the dirt. Then she looks back at us, her eyes spearing April. "Maybe it's a body. Some Halloween murder."

"Don't talk like that," Kyle says. "That's just morbid. This is all some stupid prank. At worst, there's going to be a plastic skeleton in there."

Caroline's grin turns into a sneer.

"That sounds like a challenge to me. Why don't we dig it up and find out?"

April squeezes my hand tighter and leans in, making a noise in the back of her throat so quietly I barely hear it—a tiny squeal, like that is the very last thing she wants to do.

"We're leaving," I say. I look to the boys. "Are you guys coming?"

Deshaun nods, but he doesn't move. He looks to Kyle, who's staring at the grave—or, more particularly, Caroline—with tight eyes.

"What's the matter?" Caroline taunts. "Are you scared? You wanna run home with the scaredy-cat? Oh, wait—what did we call you, April? That's right. A scaredy-*fat*." She starts saying the insult over and over, singing it like a terrible nursery rhyme while the jack-o'-lantern smiles wickedly above her.

"Come on," I say. "We don't need to stick around and listen to this."

I start to turn, but April doesn't move. She's looking at Caroline with the exact same expression as Kyle, and it's then I realize what it is: not just anger, but refusal. A refusal to be bullied.

April lets go of my hand and stalks forward, kneeling down by Caroline's side.

"Last one to find the body is a rotten egg," April says, her voice low.

She begins to dig.

For a moment I just stand there, staring at April as she fervently tosses dirt to the side—but not, I notice, at Caroline. Even now, when she's risen to Caroline's bait, she doesn't stoop to her enemy's level of cruelty. Caroline starts to dig as well, shoveling aside huge chunks of dark earth with her hands.

I look to Deshaun, and then to Kyle. I don't know what I expect from them. Maybe for Kyle to take the lead and lift April off the ground and drag her away, maybe for Deshaun to tell them both that this is stupid and we should leave.

But they don't do either of those things.

Instead, they share a look.

Kyle shrugs. Deshaun drops his head in defeat.

Then Kyle goes over to the other side of the grave and begins to dig as well.

Deshaun looks to me, defeated, and that glance tells me everything—neither he nor I wants to be here, neither he nor I wants to do this, but our friends are all in, and that means we are as well.

Besides, no one here wants Caroline to think she's won.

Deshaun and I drop to the ground beside the others and start to dig.

The dirt is cold and wet under my hands, and after a few handfuls I realize there are rocks mixed in the black soil; they cut at my skin, but I don't stop. I don't know what comes over me. It's not just wanting to look cool, not just wanting to support April. I know in this moment that I am supposed to be here, digging up a freshly churned grave, beside my friend and some relative strangers. We're all supposed to be here.

We're all supposed to be doing this.

It almost feels like we don't have a choice.

Like it's fate.

We dig for what feels like hours, until I'm coated in sweat and the night no longer seems cold and we've unearthed at least a foot of dirt. We are all hunched over, reaching down deep, pulling up chunk after chunk of soil.

Then two things happen at once.

Caroline yelps out that she's found something.

                              And the light
                    in the pumpkin
          burns out.

We all stop, the spell broken. We kneel there and pant and stare over at Caroline, who clutches something small in her hands.

"What is it?" Kyle asks. His voice is raspy, like he's just run a hundred miles.

Caroline doesn't answer. She stands up and walks away from the grave and the tombstone and the pumpkin, staring down at the box in her hands. I can barely see her silhouette in the darkened moonlight. I glance over to April. She stares at Caroline with anger clear in her eyes. Anger that Caroline won.

Whatever it is that she won.

April pushes herself to standing and we all follow, wandering over to where Caroline stands. I look just in time to see Caroline pocket something. Or maybe that's just a trick of the shadows. Before I can say anything, she turns around and tosses what she found to April.

"It's a stupid box," she says, her voice oddly tight. "Just a stupid box."

With that, she pulls a flashlight out of her pocket and flips it on. Then she stalks off into the dark grave-yard, leaving us all behind.

We gather around April and stare down at the item in her hands. Deshaun turns on his phone's flashlight and shines it down.

It's nothing.

I mean, it's *something*, but it's not anything worth burying or bringing a group of kids out into the middle of a graveyard for.

The lid of the small tin box is painted, though faded from years and years of neglect. I can barely see what it is, but it looks like . . .

"A clown," April mutters. I catch her eye. She clearly does *not* want to be holding this.

She flips open the lid of the box with trembling hands.

It's empty.

There's not even dirt inside. Just a dull silver interior rusted with age. Nothing else.

"Is that it?" Kyle asks, disappointed.

We don't say anything. We just stand there in a circle looking down at April's hands.

We're waiting for something else to happen. For this to mean something.

I have to admit—I kind of feel disappointed, and I don't really know why.

Finally, April sighs heavily and tosses the box behind her.

"Come on, guys," she says. "Let's get out of here. I'm freezing."

"Shouldn't we maybe keep that?" Deshaun asks, waving his flashlight in the direction of the tossed box.

"I don't want to have anything to do with it," April says. "In fact, I want to pretend tonight never happened."

"Fine with me," I say.

Kyle nods glumly. We're about to leave this all behind us when Deshaun's voice stops us cold.

"Guys," he says, his voice wavering.

We turn.

His flashlight illuminates the grave. Not the pit of earth we dug up. The tombstone itself. The one that had been graffitied with the words *FIND ME* only moments before.

No longer.

"Who did this?" April asks. She reaches out and grabs my dirty hand. Her palm is slicked with sweat.

"I don't know," I reply.

Kyle takes a step forward, like he's about to reach out and touch the tombstone, before stopping himself. He shakes his head.

"Maybe someone came while Caroline distracted us," he says.

"I didn't hear anything," Deshaun says. "We would have heard the spray paint."

"Maybe . . ." Kyle whispers, but he doesn't finish the sentence, because it's clear that any excuse he has is as impossible as the last.

There was no one else out here.

Just us.

Just us.

And yet, someone or some*thing* came along and changed the words on the tombstone.

The three new words send terrible chills through my bones.

YOUR NIGHTMARES BEGIN

April

I can't begin to believe what we are looking at.

YOUR NIGHTMARES BEGIN.

YOUR NIGHTMARES BEGIN.

The words echo menacingly in my head. Someone came out and painted them on the tombstone. Someone crept in behind our backs. But how? Deshaun is right—it's so quiet out here we can hear the wind rustling leaves. There's no way someone could have painted it without us hearing it. And even if they *had,* where did they go? We look around the graveyard, but no one and nothing is out there. I can't even see Caroline anymore.

We're alone.

"This is a sick joke," Kyle mutters. He doesn't sound happy about it.

"What do you think it means?" I whisper. I don't know why I ask—I don't want to know the answer.

"I think it means some high schoolers think they're pretty funny," Kyle says. "Come on. Let's get out of here before they come back and try spray-painting *us*."

He turns from the grave and begins to walk away. Deshaun doesn't move, and neither do Andres or I. I share a look with Andres. *I knew we shouldn't have come out here*, I want to say. In that moment, I want to yell at him. Because coming here was all his idea. Because I would have happily stayed at home and not had anything to do with the stupid note and this stupid prank.

Caroline's taunts are still ringing in my ears, louder than the words painted on the tombstone. I want to throw something. Break something. I want to scream and cry and kick.

I do nothing.

It's only when Andres touches my arm that I realize I'm clenching my hands, white-knuckled and shaking.

"He's right," Andres says, looking after Kyle. "We should go."

"Yeah," Deshaun says. "I'm freezing."

My rage makes me so hot I can't feel the cold, but I know Andres is right. Just as I know Kyle is right. This was all a stupid prank, and Caroline was just being her usual horrible self, and the sooner I am home and in bed, the happier I will be. Because then I can pretend tonight never happened. I can pretend Andres and I went to bed after watching stupid movies and eating too much candy and popcorn. I can pretend this was all a bad dream.

But first, I'll need to wash the dirt from my hands.

And get that clown out of my head.

"Do you think we should cover it back up?" Deshaun asks, gesturing toward where I threw the stupid tin.

I shake my head.

"I want to go home," I say.

Andres squeezes my hand.

We follow Kyle back down the hill and out of the graveyard. I don't look back. Not once.

Not until we reach the gate, when I can't take it anymore—it feels like I'm being watched—and I look over my shoulder.

There is a light in the cemetery. Candlelight.
Jack-o'-lantern light.

The pumpkin has been relit.

And I swear, in the darkness, I see a shape illuminated in the harsh orange glow.

A figure.

Waving at us as we flee.

Not just a figure.

A clown.

Caroline

By the time I've made it home, I'm shaking. And it's not from the cold and it's not from my shock at seeing stupid April and her stupid friends in the stupid graveyard.

It's from the stupid tin box.

I storm into my room and slam the door. I don't care if my dad hears me. It's not like he's going to come in and yell at me. I could throw a party in here and he wouldn't care, just as long as he thought it was something that made me *happy*. If it was helping me *cope*.

Please.

I rip off my coat and throw it in the corner, two

small pieces of paper crumpled and clenched tight in my palms.

Someone is messing with me.

Someone is trying to play a prank.

Well, *I'm* not going to fall for it. No one messes with me. No one.

I thump down in front of my bedroom mirror and stare at my reflection. My eyes are red. Was I crying?

No.

Definitely not crying.

It was just the cold air. The wind.

The anger.

I bet April had something to do with this. Her and her stupid friends. They're the ones who dragged me out to the cemetery. They're the ones who wrote the note and planted the box.

But how did they know?

How did they know?

I unclench my fists one at a time and drop the crumpled papers on the floor in front of me. For a while I just stare at them, my breath hot in my chest. I can't believe someone would try to pull this.

She's going to pay.

They're all going to pay.

I reach out and grab one of the papers. My hand trembles. From anger. From so much *anger*.

It's the note I found in my locker this afternoon. A handwriting I can't place.

I'M WAITING FOR YOU, SUNNYBUNNY. MIDNIGHT. OLD CEMETERY.

No one else calls me that. No one else has ever heard that name besides my dad, and there's absolutely no way he wrote this note or had anything to do with tonight.

I stare at the note for a long time.

I want to burn it. Bury it. Rip it into a thousand pieces.

Instead, I pick it up and crumple it once more, then toss it in my trash can.

The other . . .

I stare at the other piece of paper for a long time. Until my eyes hurt and I swear I can hear my dad snoring in the other room. Until it feels like the shadows are closing in and my room is shrinking and I'm falling, falling . . .

Then I shake my head and force myself to stand, grabbing the paper as I go.

I yank open my nightstand drawer. Toss the paper inside. Slam it shut.

I turn off the lights.

Close my eyes.

But even as night closes in, I still see the image bright as day.

The photo I should never have found in the graveyard.

The reminder of what should have been buried a year ago.

PART TWO
the
nightmares

Deshaun

I normally don't have any trouble falling asleep.

Clearly, Kyle doesn't either, and tonight's no exception—he's snoring on the floor beside me, one arm flung over his head. He passed out a few minutes after we got home. He didn't want to talk about what happened in the graveyard. I couldn't blame him. I didn't want to talk about it either.

Trouble is, not talking about the events doesn't mean I can stop thinking about them. Almost an hour after Kyle passed out, here I am, lying in bed and replaying everything on loop, trying to find the moment when someone might have come in and spray-painted the tombstone. Trying to understand what—if anything—Caroline found in the tin. Trying to figure out why, of all places, it had to have been the graveyard. As if the person leaving the notes knew.

An hour later, I still don't have any answers.

Another hour later, I really, really wish I could talk to someone about it.

If only to get it out of my head.

I don't want to wake up Kyle, though. He's my best friend, and we talk about everything. But I know when he doesn't want to talk about stuff, when he needs time, and I know that if I push it he'll only take longer to open up. Like when I tried to get him to come out before he was ready. He didn't speak to me for two weeks. (Then we talked again, and it was fine. And when he was ready to tell everyone else, I was there for him.)

If only I had April's number. Or Andres's. Not that I expect either of them to be awake right now— at least, I *hope* they're not awake right now—but maybe texting them would feel like saying the words I want to say out loud. Maybe it would help me sleep.

Maybe it would keep me from thinking about ghosts. About open graves.

A few years ago, I was playing hide-and-seek with some kids that I thought were my friends. It was late. Dark. And it was Halloween. They'd wanted to play in the graveyard, and I went along with them. Except, after a while of playing, I'd found a really great hiding spot. And they never found me. And I never found my way out.

I spent all night in the graveyard.

Alone.

Except I hadn't been alone. I'd heard things out there.

Felt things.

Seen things. Things that even today give me nightmares.

And I know, in the bottom of my heart, that it wasn't a person who spray-painted that tombstone or left the tin box.

There's no way anyone else was out there, I tell myself. *It had to have been a ghost. Or poltergeist. We were brought there for a reason, and it definitely,* definitely, *wasn't good.*

But that's only part of what I want to say. The rest I don't want to say aloud. I don't want to admit to anyone else, let alone myself.

We dug something up in that graveyard. And I've seen enough scary movies to know that digging something up in a graveyard leads to only one thing:

Being haunted.

I stare up into the corners of my room, and I swear that the shadows are staring back.

I shudder.

It's not my imagination.

The shadows *are* staring back.

Just like they had been in the graveyard. Tonight, and all those years ago.

The room suddenly goes as cold as a freezer; my breath comes out in a cloud.

I

    am

        not

            alone.

I don't blink.

I don't breathe.

Because I know if I do, I will see something, and right now, I don't want to see anything.

I want to fall asleep.

I want this to go away.

I want it all to be a bad dream.

I want—

The desktop computer in my room flickers on.

At first I think it's my imagination, or maybe some sort of weird electrical surge, but then the screen is filled with blinking lights and a crackle that almost sounds like static and almost sounds like fire, and worst of all, even though he's passed out right next to it, Kyle doesn't wake up at all.

I stare at the screen, transfixed, as the lights whirl around, becoming shapes. Eight-bit shapes that almost look like people. A landscape that is nothing but pale green covered in gray blobs. The screen continues to change and shift and sharpen and the noises become less static and more like wind. And then I realize what I'm looking at.

Five shapes. Five people.

Five people around a mound of dirt.

Five people around a grave.

It's us.

No, I want to yell out. But I can't say a word. I can't move a muscle. I am paralyzed, glued to my bed, and even though Kyle is right there, he might as well be a million miles away.

I watch as the figures dig at the grave.

I watch as one of them pulls out a small pixel to the sound of victorious music.

And I watch as the figure opens what they've found.

The screen instantly changes, inverting to black figures and a background so white and bright my eyes hurt. I don't close my eyes. I couldn't blink if I wanted to. I don't even think my heart is beating.

Something is coming out of that one tiny unearthed pixel.

A blob.

A figure.

A ghost.

It pulls itself from the box, growing larger and larger on the screen, eating up the white, spreading over the screen like spilled ink on paper.

Devouring the light.

Growing larger.

Coming nearer.

And the only sound,

the only sound,

is static.

Static.

The shadow has filled the screen now.

A shadow with blazing white eyes

and sharp white teeth.
It reaches the edges of the screen.
It presses
out.
The screen bulges.
Static roars.
And I know
—I know—
that it is coming for us
for me.
Whatever we unearthed has found us.
I want to scream.
I want to run.
I want to hide my eyes
as the shadow
grows.
As the shadow reaches *out*
from the TV
becomes a hand
a hand stretching
into my bedroom
five
gnarled
claws.

I call out to Kyle as the hand reaches for him
as it looms over his face.
I have to save him.
"Kyle," I croak again.
Barely a whisper.
Barely a breath.
"Kyle," purrs a voice.
Not mine.
Not mine.
The talons begin to close
around Kyle's face.
He's going to suffocate
He's going to—
Kyle rolls over then, and as he does, he knocks his
arm into the computer tower, making the whole unit
shake. One of my old toy cars falls off and thuds to
the ground with a loud crash, startling him awake.
Startling me.
"Wha—?" Kyle snorts. He sits up. His eyes are
still closed.
I jolt. Finally able to move.
But I can't stop staring at the computer. At the
turned-off computer.

My skin vibrates and hums like I've been charged with electricity.

I open my mouth.

"Kyle—" I say, louder this time.

But Kyle flops back down. Already snoring.

I don't move. Even as feeling and blood rush back to my fingers.

I don't stop watching the computer. Waiting for it to turn on again.

Wondering if I had been dreaming, one of those half-waking dreams, and Kyle had woken me up. Wondering if I'm losing my mind.

I watch the computer all night.

I watch it until the sky outside melts from black to pink and my eyes burn.

Only then do I let myself close my eyes. Only then do I let myself go to sleep.

When I do, I dream of static.

April

My mouth feels like it's filled with static when I wake up.

I don't open my eyes or get out of bed right away, though. I lie there, curled up under all my covers, and try to sort through everything that happened last night. Andres snores loudly on the floor beside my bed—he normally stays in my little brother's room, but I asked him to stay in mine. I didn't want to be alone.

I could tell he didn't want to be alone either.

We'd all practically jogged back to our houses in silence. We hadn't even said goodnight when we parted from Kyle and Deshaun. We just shared a look, one that said we weren't ever going to talk about this again, and left.

I almost wish we'd talked about it.

What in the world had Caroline seen in that tin? Did she take something from it? Was it all her doing? I wanted to blame her for it, but seeing the shock on her face, the way her pale skin went even whiter, made me think that she was just as surprised as we were. Whatever she had seen had been personal. Which meant she hadn't just followed us here—someone had buried that tin for her to find, which meant she probably got a note as well. Someone had wanted all five of us in that graveyard. But why?

Despite the layers, I shiver with a sudden chill at the thought of what I saw when we were leaving. A silhouette by the grave. A clown.

I mean, it had to be a clown. It had a pale shirt with poofy shoulders and fuzzy hair that looked like an upturned crescent moon. It waved at me with a giant gloved hand. And I swear I'd seen its eyes. Glowing pale blue in the dark. Illuminating a smile way too big for a normal human face . . .

Another shiver.

No. It had to be my imagination.

And even if it wasn't, it was just some high school kid in a costume. Probably the same one who brought us all out there. They probably recorded the whole thing and put it up online to make fun of us—*look at the kids who scared themselves in a graveyard.*

But . . . really, nothing too scary had happened out there.

Except for the clown.

How could they have known about the clown?

It doesn't make sense. If it was someone pulling a prank, why didn't they jump out and scare us? Why was it so silent?

Maybe something went wrong. A prop didn't work. Maybe there was supposed to be a plastic skeleton or something that popped out of the grave.

(Though what if it wasn't kids? What if it was the clown?)

The more I lie here and think about it, though, the less sense it makes. Why were we all brought out there? What had been watching us leave?

I hear Mom moving about in the room beside mine. Will she be upset that Andres stayed in my room even though he's gay? Maybe I should kick him out before she notices, make him sneak over to Freddy's room. I can tell Freddy isn't up yet. He's a terror in the morning—when he's awake, you know it.

I'm smiling as I think of how Freddy would wake Andres up with his own "good morning" song—but the smile goes away as soon as I hear something strange . . . something falling over with a soft shuffle.

It sounds closer than my mom's room. It sounds—

No.

It sounds like it's coming from my closet.

I freeze. I stare at the closed closet door and I know I couldn't move even if I wanted to.

I still hear Andres asleep on the floor, which should make me feel safe, but it doesn't. Because it seems like besides his breathing, everything else in the world has gone silent.

No birds chirping their morning hellos.

No cars buzzing past.

No Mom making coffee or starting breakfast.

Silent.

Save for the shuffling

     coming

          from

              my

                 closet.

Something else falls, like a coat crumpling to the ground, and I hear a sound that makes my blood run cold.

A giggle.

The same maniacal giggle I heard last night. In the graveyard.

Another shuffle. Another giggle.

"April," comes a high-pitched man's voice, followed by another blood-chilling giggle. "I know where you sleep, April. I can see you . . ."

A squeak.

And the door

      slowly

            opens.

"I see you, April," comes the man's voice. And through the crack in the door, I see the pale blue eye glowing like a moon, the sharp teeth like a snake's. The clown's voice deepens, grows so loud I feel my bed shake.

"I SEE YOU."

The door flings open.

I close my eyes and scream.

"April!" someone yells.

Not the clown. Not the clown.

Someone is on my bed. Someone's hands grip my shoulders. I scream again.

"April!" the voice says again. No, not the clown's voice. Andres. "April, it's okay! It's just me. You had a bad dream."

He wraps his arms around me in a hug. Squeezes me tight. And it's only then that I realize I am crying. I can barely breathe. Can barely hear him over the blood pounding in my ears.

He holds me close, and I finally open my eyes.

Stare at the closet door.

The closed closet door.

But no.

It's open,

just a little bit.

Just enough for someone to watch us sleep.

And I know I closed it before going to bed.

Kyle

I don't know what has Deshaun so freaked out. He heads downstairs the moment he sees I'm awake, and there's no chance of me asking him anything with his parents there. We eat our breakfast cereal in silence while his mom and dad talk about some of their favorite Halloween costumes over the years. Deshaun barely pays them any attention—he keeps glancing at the TV over in the living room, his dark skin paling with every glance.

Finally, he suggests we get out of the house. Go throw a football around. Which is definitely strange, because he's always been the type to suggest staying indoors and playing video games over going out and playing sports.

"What happened last night?" I ask as we head toward the school playground.

"I don't know," he says. "We went to the graveyard and—"

"Not the graveyard," I interrupt. "After. Why were you so freaked out this morning?"

He looks like he's going to ignore me. Change the subject or something. He keeps tossing the ball to himself, looking everywhere but at me. He seems spooked. Every single Halloween decoration we pass makes him start, even the stupid jack-o'-lanterns grinning on the neighbor's porch. Like he's seeing ghosts. Everywhere.

Years ago, he admitted to me that he was terrified of ghosts. This came, of course, after we'd watched a movie about a poltergeist and he'd spent the entire time clutching a blanket to his chin, petrified. He hadn't slept that night, and had asked me to stay over the next night as well. I could tell he was worried I'd make fun of him. I didn't, of course. And we haven't watched a truly scary ghost movie since.

"I . . ." he finally says. "I . . . I mean, did you wake up at all last night? Did you hear anything?"

The way he says it makes fear roil inside my gut, sour and sick.

I don't think I dreamed at all last night, and I definitely don't remember waking up in the middle of the night.

"I didn't hear anything," I tell him. "I slept like a rock."

He bites his lip.

"Then I . . . I guess I had a bad dream."

I can tell by the way he says it that he doesn't quite believe it, and I don't believe it either. We've had more sleepovers than I can count, and we've both had bad dreams while staying at each other's places. But I've never seen him this freaked.

"What was it?" I ask quietly.

He just shakes his head and walks faster. When we reach the field and start tossing the ball back and forth, he doesn't mention anything else about last night. About the graveyard or the bad dream or whatever it was. I can tell he's thinking about it from the distracted look in his eyes and the way he keeps fumbling the ball.

But I don't bring it up.

Whatever happened truly scared him, and for some reason, that has me scared more than anything else.

Andres

I don't know what's gotten into April.

Ever since she woke up screaming from her nightmare, she's been silent. I've only seen her like this a few other times, when she was super upset or scared after an unexpectedly scary movie. But try as I might, I can't get her to tell me what's wrong. She doesn't speak all through breakfast. I mean, she does, but not about anything important. We just ask her mom about work and trick-or-treat last night and her mom asks what we watched on TV. Nothing remotely important.

April's jumpy too. When Freddy comes down, still wearing his T. rex costume, he lets out a loud roar that makes me giggle. April yelps and jumps in her seat, spilling her cereal all over the place. Her mom rushes over and helps clean everything up.

"I'm really scary!" Freddy yells happily.

"Yes, you are," his mom agrees.

April barely responds.

We make it through breakfast, and then April says she wants to go for a walk to get some fresh air. I grab my shoes and follow her outside.

Clearly she's upset—she doesn't even change out of her pajamas, just throws a coat on top.

The neighborhood feels strange today. Like it's waking from some scary dream. The lawns are still covered in Halloween decorations, but in the light of day, they all seem . . . fake. The fabric ghosts hanging from trees that looked so creepy last night are limp and lifeless. The plastic skeletons on porches seem especially plastic. And the trees that had seemed like taloned hands are just normal, bare trees. It's hard to imagine what got us so creeped out.

Which makes me wonder . . .

"What's going on?" I ask April when I realize where we're heading. "Are we going back?"

I don't have to say where. She knows exactly what I'm talking about.

"I have to see," she says, almost to herself. She doesn't slow down, and the look on her face concerns me.

"April, why are we going back there?"

"Because . . ."

She shudders and falls silent.

I reach out and take her arm. My touch is gentle, but she still jerks back like she doesn't realize it's me.

"Sorry," I say quickly, dropping my hand. "It's just . . . you seem strange today. Like. I don't know. Did something happen?"

"I don't want to talk about it," she says.

That hits harder than a slap to the face. We talk about everything. *Everything.* So why is she suddenly acting like I'm her enemy?

"Okay," I say. "But, just . . . why are we heading back there?"

She doesn't answer, just keeps walking.

I don't try asking her again.

It doesn't take long for us to reach the graveyard, especially not at the pace she's setting.

This, too, looks so much different in the day. Birds swoop through the skies and sing from tree branches. A few cars wind through the single paved road that curves through the entire graveyard—families paying their respects. April doesn't bother taking the sidewalk or the road. She cuts straight across the grass, following the same path we took last night. Toward one of the small hills, this one topped with a gnarled tree.

I don't know what she's looking for and a part of me doesn't want to find it. I don't like graveyards during the best of times, and after what happened last night—and with the scary way April's acting—today isn't the best of times. I want to get out of here as soon as possible. I want us to go back to her place and put on a comedy show or something and push all of this out of our minds.

Halloween is over. Last night is over.

I really, really want this to be over.

I'm also wondering if I should have brought the baseball bat, because the way April looks at everything with fear in her eyes makes me think she doesn't believe this is over by a long shot.

"This can't be right," April mutters.

We near the top of the hill. It's definitely the one from last night—the same knobbly tree, the same faded tombstone. Only now . . .

"What happened to the grave?" I ask.

Because the grass here is green and lush and covered in red leaves. There's no grinning jack-o'-lantern, and the grave itself is wiped clean. No sign of spray paint. No carved *DO NOT DISTURB*. No sign of anything.

"Maybe we're in the wrong place?" she says. She glances around. But from here, we can see the entire small graveyard, and it's clear that we're on the right hill. I don't tell her that, though, because she's already off. Down the hill and over to the next.

This one has no tree. And no sign of a recently dug grave. This tombstone looks even more weathered than the last.

April makes an aggravated noise in her throat and heads over to the next hill.

We comb the graveyard for what feels like hours, but is probably only twenty minutes. We don't find anything. Not a trace that anyone—including us—was here last night.

April finally storms toward a bench and sits down. I follow her, but I don't sit. I don't know if she wants me close, or even around. She looks so upset.

"April—"

"What happened last night?" she interrupts. "What did we *do* last night?"

She starts to cry.

I sit down beside her and put my arm over her shoulders. She leans into me and cries harder.

"What did we do?" she asks again, softer this time.

"We went out because some high school kids tricked us," I say tentatively. "They left a weird tin box as a prank and something probably went wrong because it wasn't all that scary, and then we went home, and—"

"No," she says. "No, that wasn't a prank. I know it. Last night, I saw something. In my room. In the closet. *Watching us.*"

My skin immediately goes cold.

"What?"

She doesn't answer. Just sniffs louder and cries harder, her whole body shaking against me.

"April," I say slowly, softly. "What do you mean, someone was in your room? Who? *How?*"

She shakes her head against my chest.

"I don't know. I was so scared."

"Why didn't you wake me up?"

"I couldn't move. I couldn't even breathe."

My mind races. Someone was in her room. Worse, in her closet. I was *sleeping* beside her closet. How did I not wake up? How had we not seen anything this morning? I mean, even if someone *had* crept in while we were away, they wouldn't have been able to stay in the closet all night.

"Maybe it was Freddy," I say. "Maybe he put on a costume to scare us."

"No. No, it wasn't him. It was . . ."

She can't finish her sentence.

I hold her there and try to think of something comforting to say but I can't find the words.

"Maybe it was a nightmare," I say. "You know, one of those waking ones. Maybe you just thought you were awake. I had that happen once. I thought there was a vampire in my closet and I hid under the covers for an hour before—"

"It wasn't a dream!" she yells. "And it wasn't Freddy! I don't know what it was, but I know . . . I know it had to do with what happened last night."

"Last night was just a stupid prank."

"No, it wasn't. You wouldn't understand."

"I'm trying," I say. I really am. But I don't know

how she expects me to believe that there was, what? A monster in her closet? One that only she could see?

She looks at me for a moment and I look away; I'm worried she can see my doubts behind my eyes.

She stands up.

"I hope you never understand," she says solemnly. "You don't want to know what fear like that feels like."

Then she turns and stomps off down the hill.

I watch her go.

It's clear she doesn't want me to follow.

Kyle

Deshaun doesn't open up at all for the rest of the morning. Seriously, it's like trying to talk to a brick wall. I keep trying to gently ask him what he dreamed about or what he thought happened in the graveyard, but the moment I even get close to the subject, he clams up. It's frustrating. I want to talk to *someone* about the graveyard. I want to know what Deshaun dreamed, what scared him so much. Mainly because I can't remember my dreams, and for some reason, that feels more dangerous than a nightmare.

I also don't want to go home.

We toss the ball about for an hour and talk about everything except for what I think we should be talking about. It's starting to annoy me, honestly. Not because Deshaun is being quiet. Not because he jumps at every gust of wind or snapped branch. But because he won't let me help him. He's standing twenty feet away, but we might as well be on different planets.

I'm about to suggest we head in to grab a snack from a café when I see him.

The boy from last night. Andres.

He's walking along the side of the field, hands in his pockets and head down, slouched over in a puffy coat and hat.

Deshaun tosses the ball and it lands at my feet.

"Hey!" I call out, waving. Andres jolts and looks up at me. It seems to take a moment for him to realize who we are. Then he smiles and jogs over.

"Hey, guys," he says when he nears.

"Hey," Deshaun says. He pauses, and his voice grows uncertain. "Where's April?"

Andres's smile drops. "Home," he says.

He looks like he wants to say more, but stays silent.

"Gotcha," Deshaun says. "What are you up to?"

Andres swallows hard. He glances behind himself. "Just getting some fresh air."

"Well, um," I say. I don't know why talking is so hard right now. "Did you want to hang out or something? I think we were going to go to the café."

"No, it's okay," he says quickly. "I'm just . . . I'm just going to head home."

We barely say goodbye before he turns away and walks off the field. Deshaun and I watch him go, and for the first time this morning, it actually feels like Deshaun and I are here together.

"What's gotten into him?" Deshaun asks.

I turn from Andres and look toward the way he was coming from. My breath catches when I realize where he was.

I don't answer Deshaun, but I think I know.

Andres was in the graveyard.

April

I don't know what's worse: the fact that there was a terrifying clown in my closet or the fact that Andres doesn't believe me. I mean, I know he didn't *say* he doesn't believe me, but I can tell he doesn't. The trouble is, I don't think I'd believe it either if I hadn't been the one seeing it. Just remembering the glowing eyes, the rumbling voice . . . I shudder.

The clown *was* real.

It followed me home from the graveyard, and now there isn't even a trace of the weird tombstone or grave to prove it.

My fear turns to anger in a heartbeat. I've only been angry at Andres a few times in the past, but this time it hits me like a burst of fire in my veins. *He's* the one who dragged me out to the graveyard in the first place. He *saw* the writing on the tombstone and the creepy tin. *He's* the reason all of this happened. And yet, he has the nerve to think I'm making something like this up?

I storm away from the graveyard. I don't know where I'm going but I just know I don't want to be around Andres right now because if I am, I'll say something mean. This is his fault. *His fault.*

I know that the only reason I'm so angry is because I'm tired and terrified, but knowing that doesn't make the rage inside me any less real.

I walk through the downtown, the remnants of last night's trick-or-treat strewn about everywhere. Long strands of toilet paper drape across cars from high schoolers playing pranks. Jack-o'-lanterns—some in one piece, some smashed to bits on the concrete—line every sidewalk. Ghosts and ghouls hang from the eaves overlooking storefronts and candy is scattered about like confetti. A few adults are outside, sweeping up the debris or slowly putting away décor. But for the most part, the downtown is empty. Sleepy. Just like always.

Except, some stores have mannequins outside dressed in costumes, like witches and goblins and even . . . clowns.

I slow down.

A clown mannequin stands outside of the post office.

I don't remember there being a clown mannequin there yesterday.

Or the day before.

I would have noticed.

It isn't at all like the clown I saw in the graveyard or in my room. At least, I don't think it is. But as I get closer, I start to feel cold. My feet are heavy, and I don't want to walk anywhere closer to it.

The trouble is, I can't stop walking.

The clown has giant poofy red hair and a painted smile from ear to ear and paint around his eyes. His costume is striped and satin and he wears giant red shoes and giant white gloves. Even though it's a mannequin and even though I'm sure it is nothing at all like the clown I saw, something still hooks in my chest, a fear that tells me this *is* the clown from the graveyard.

My feet lead me closer.

I don't want to go closer.

I force myself to keep my eyes straight ahead as I pass by. The chill gets worse. I force myself to keep my breathing slow and calm and my footsteps measured, because it is sunny outside and nothing bad or scary happens when it is sunny outside.

I walk past the clown.

And its eyes

    follow

        me.

I jolt and turn around. But the mannequin clown is staring straight ahead and its eyes are nothing more than paint and there's absolutely no way it was staring at me. But I know it was watching me. I know it from the way my heart pounds and fear trickles down the back of my throat.

I turn and hurry the rest of the way home.

Kyle

"Kyle, honey?" Mom calls out from the kitchen.

It's almost dinnertime, and I knew I couldn't hold off on coming home any longer. I'd asked Deshaun if he wanted me to stay over again, pitching it as an opportunity to do a video game binge rather than a way to keep him from being afraid of his room, but he refused. Said he was too tired. And he looked it, too, but he also didn't look like he wanted to be alone. After spending all day hanging out, I hadn't gotten any closer to understanding why he was so upset and distant.

"Hey, Mom," I say. I take off my shoes and start heading up to my room.

"Honey . . ." she says, and I know from the tone in her voice that something is wrong.

And I know what that *something* is even before I hear his voice.

"Where the heck were you?" Dad grumbles.

My gut drops to my feet.

It's Saturday. Which means Dad is home from work. I'd forgotten. Or at least I'd *wanted* to forget. I'd wanted to just block him out of my mind altogether.

Maybe I should have been more insistent about staying at Deshaun's.

"Out," I say.

Dad stomps into the entryway. His footsteps actually make the pictures rattle in their frames. Great. He's already in a bad mood.

"Don't you talk to me like that," he growls.

I stare up at him. He's gruff and covered in facial hair and his greasy hair is slicked back. He's in his forties but he looks older than my grandpa. I don't know why my mom is still married to him.

"I'm sorry, sir," I say. I do my best to pitch my voice to sound sincere. I don't want to get into a screaming match with him right now. I have way too much other stuff on my mind.

"I'll show you sorry," he says. He looks me up and down. "Go wash up and be back down in ten for dinner. You look terrible."

I bite my tongue to keep myself from saying that he looks worse than I do. I turn and head up the steps.

Dad watches me as I go. Then he calls out when I'm halfway there.

"Maybe I'll have you clean out the snake tanks later."

My gut twists in anger. He knows I hate his snakes. He knows I can't stand looking at them and really can't stand living with them. Even if they are all locked up in the basement.

"They're *your* snakes," I mutter beneath my breath.

"What did you say?" Dad yells.

I stop and turn. My chest is a mix of heat and acid, anger and fear. I *hate* him. So much. And I hate that no matter how much I hate him, it doesn't change a thing. He's still here. I'm still stuck with him.

All it does is make it worse for me.

I should just shut up and not talk. I should apologize and head up the stairs and wash up and maybe if I'm lucky we'll pretend this never happened.

He thunders up the steps so fast I don't even have time to turn and face him. All I feel is his hand on the back of my neck as he grabs me. Then I'm weightless, just for a moment, before he drops me hard. I land on my feet, but I'm shaking.

"Don't you ever!" he yells, his breath reeking. "Don't you *ever* speak back to me!"

I hear my mom saying something below us. Dad pulls away.

"Get to your room," he commands. "And stay there. No dinner for you. Not until you learn how to speak to your elders."

He stomps back down the steps, pounding his fist against the wall as he goes. I don't look back. I don't wait on the steps either. Instead, I run up to my room as he storms down to the basement.

Maybe it's my imagination, but I swear the moment he opens the basement door, I hear them hissing.

And I swear they're hissing for me.

Andres

By dinnertime, I still haven't heard from April. That worries me, and it also hurts. She doesn't have a reason to be angry at me. I mean, would she believe me if I said I saw a zombie walrus walking around my bedroom? She'd think I'd eaten too much candy.

Pride keeps me from texting her. But it doesn't mean I feel good about it.

Tomorrow, if she still hasn't said anything, I'll apologize. I hate having her mad at me.

I've spent most of the day hanging out at home with my brothers, playing video games and watching my phone. After dinner, I try watching a movie to get my mind off of things. It doesn't work.

So I do what I usually do when I'm stressed out, which happens more than it should and is why I get headaches sometimes.

I take a bubble bath.

Cheesy, maybe, but I don't really care. It helps. Mom buys the really nice bubble bath soap, so it smells good too. And we've got a really big tub.

When the tub is full of hot water and the bubbles tower at least a foot over the rim, I hop in, trying not to yelp at how hot it is.

I close my eyes and sink down into the bath. I tune out the thud of footsteps as my brothers run around the house, chasing each other in a last-ditch effort to avoid bed. They're almost all younger than me, and they've definitely eaten every single piece of candy they got yesterday. If anyone gets any sleep tonight, I'll be amazed. I guess we just have to wait for the sugar crash.

Maybe tomorrow I'll head over to April's with donuts as my way of apologizing. Maybe she'll come around and realize she was worked up over nothing.

My thoughts drift.

I didn't expect to run into Kyle and Deshaun

today. I'd barely seen Deshaun before, and had never seen Kyle. Now we were running into each other at the park. Weird.

Did they go to the graveyard after I left? Did they learn that the unburied grave was no longer there? That something truly strange was going on? Probably not. They looked so happy, playing catch, like nothing was wrong. Like we hadn't all met in a graveyard last night and been spooked half to death.

The bath warms through my veins, makes my thoughts heavy and sluggish. I let myself drift . . .

Something brushes my leg.

I jolt. My eyes open.

Is it my imagination, or did the bubbles move?

"You're being ridiculous," I whisper to myself. I try to relax. The water is lukewarm. Huh. How did it already get so cool? Maybe I fell asleep?

I sidle back down into the bubbles. Close my eyes.

And something cold and rough rubs against my leg.

I jerk. Water splashes over the side of the tub and my heart feels like it's in my throat. *What was that?* It almost felt like there was something in the tub.

"It's just your imagination," I tell myself.

But just as I'm about to sink back into the tub for
the third time
      the bubbles
            move.
Fear freezes me as I understand.
I am not alone in the tub.
Something is there.
     At my feet.
Something is there and I can't move and as I open
my mouth to call out for help
           it emerges.
Slicing up through the bubbles.
A gray triangle.
     A shark's fin.
It rises steadily, bigger and bigger, and I know
soon it will surface and I will feel the cold, rough skin
of it just before it opens its jaws, and my mother will
come in and see me about to be eaten, and it's only
then, when I think of my mother, think of her shocked
face, that I am able to move.
Before it surfaces.
Before I feel its teeth chomp into me.
I manage to push myself from the tub. I leap. Out
onto the bath mat. I grab my towel and wrap it around

me and run out into the hallway, slamming the door behind me.

"Andres is naked," Leo says, giggling from his doorway.

I blush and quickly run to my room.

"What was that?" I whisper as I sit there, dripping, on the edge of my bed.

I don't go back into the bathroom to find out.

Finally, when I'm so cold I'm shivering, I change into pajamas. From the other side of the hall, I hear my mother thud toward me. Hear her knock on the bathroom door, and when no one answers—even though I want to call out to her not to go in there—I hear the bathroom door open.

"Andres!" she calls out. "You forgot to drain the tub!"

She can't reach in there! She can't!

I yank open my door and run over to the bathroom.

Just in time to see her reach elbow deep into the bubble-less water.

Just in time to see her pull out the plug and stand, shaking her head at me disapprovingly.

"You need to learn to be more responsible," she says.

I watch the water drain.
There is nothing in the tub.
Nothing.
But try as I might, I can't convince myself that it was all a bad dream.

Deshaun

There's a large part of me that wants to invite Kyle over again. Even though he was starting to annoy me with all of his not-so-subtle questions, the moment I step inside my room, fear trickles down my spine.

I stand in the doorway of my bedroom, frozen, staring at the remains of last night. The mound of blankets that Kyle had been sleeping on. The bag of half-eaten candy. And the blank computer screen. Sitting there like it's the most normal thing in the world.

Even with the sounds of my family moving about downstairs and cleaning up after dinner, my room feels isolated and silent and cold, like it exists in the far reaches of the Arctic. My family feels thousands of miles away.

Maybe I *should* text Kyle. But no, I don't want to be the annoying friend who always wants to hang out.

I do all the things I normally do before bed. This time, after brushing my teeth, I don't turn on the computer to play video games. I prepare for the dark.

I've read a lot of books and watched a lot of movies. I might not know *what* we're dealing with, but I'm prepared to deal with almost anything.

I form a ring of salt around my bed to protect me, a thick white line on my hardwood floor; I just have to remember to clean it up before my parents wake up in the morning. I light some incense that the package says is for "purification and protection" and hope my parents don't smell it and think I'm burning the house down. Tomorrow I'm going to try to get some holy water. And maybe garlic, though I don't think it's a vampire. I just want to have all my bases covered.

I throw a blanket over my computer and unplug it. To be safe.

When I've done everything I can think of, I sit there, as uncomfortably as possible to keep myself awake, and read a sci-fi book, and nothing happens.

I mean, nothing has happened all day. No moved objects. No mysterious voices. No writing on the wall. It has my nerves on edge. All day, I've been able to think of nothing but what we released last night, and what it wanted, and what it was waiting for. Because if I was a ghost, that would be precisely what I'd do to my victim—I'd make them think that they were safe, that it was all their imagination. And once I had them certain everything was okay again, I'd strike.

I swallow hard. Everything seems okay *right now*.

So why is nothing striking?

I refocus on my book.

The words seem to swim on the page. My eyes are heavy, and my head throbs from all the bright lights. Maybe I could rest for just a moment. Get rid of the headache.

Words dance. My eyes flutter closed. It can't hurt. Just for a moment.

"Deshauuunnnn."

I snap open my eyes.

I nearly yelp.

Everything in my room is rearranged.

My closet door is open and all my clothes are on the ground.

My toys have all been turned upside down.

My posters now face the walls.

Everything, *everything*, has been changed. How is that possible? I didn't even fall asleep. I should have heard something. I should have . . .

My heart hammers loudly in my ears. I set down my book.

I crawl
    to the edge
        of my bed.

And look down.

To the ring of salt protecting me.

The ring of salt that *should* have been protecting me.

Only it's no longer a ring.

It's been broken.

No, not broken—
        rearranged
    into four words, crisp white and
      bold on the wooden floor.

NOTHING CAN STOP ME.

Caroline

Every time I close my eyes, I see her face.
Every time I close my eyes, I choke on dirt.
I stop closing my eyes.
I sit in the dark and wait.

April

I know I'm supposed to be angry at Andres. But as I lie in my bed, comforter pulled up to my chin, I stare at the open closet door with fear hammering in my veins, and I want nothing more than for him to be here with me. Even if he doesn't believe me, even if he thinks I'm losing my mind or making things up, at least it's another person here. Another person between me and the clown.

I convince myself that if I have someone else here, the clown can't get me.

That's how it always works in horror movies, right? The evil monster only targets victims when they're alone?

Right now, I'm alone.

Right now, I feel like I am in the perfect spot to be a victim.

I can hear my mom getting ready for bed in the bathroom. I can hear Freddy's audiobook nursery rhyme playing, putting him to sleep. I can hear every creak and groan of our old house.

What I can't hear is the clown.

That scares me more than anything.

After that weird incident downtown, which I've convinced myself was all in my head anyway, the day was quiet. Too quiet. I played video games with Freddy. Ate more candy than I should have. Did my homework. Watched a movie with Mom. And through it all, I was very aware that *something* should have been going wrong. I was being hunted by a phantom clown, right? So why was everything normal?

Why was it that every time I closed my eyes, I felt like I was back in the graveyard?

By nightfall, the stress of not seeing anything was getting worse. Because by nightfall, I'd started to second-guess myself. I'd started to understand why Andres would have such a hard time believing me.

After a day of not seeing the clown, I was beginning to believe that maybe what I saw last night *was* a dream. A stress dream carried over from a stressful night in a creepy graveyard. Completely understandable. Completely rational—much more so than a phantom clown.

And yet, now that I'm here, in my bed, in the dark, all that rational logic is swallowed by fear.

What if I'm *not* making it up?

What if the clown only comes out at night?

What if the clown is only toying with me?

Making me think it isn't real so I'll let my guard down.

Waiting for the perfect moment to strike.

I swallow, and I'm so alert I can hear even that small noise.

Down the hall, Mom closes her bedroom door with a click.

Freddy's audiobook starts playing a faint nursery rhyme, filled with children laughing and jingling bells.

Bells.

I clutch the comforter tighter.

I hear jingle bells.

Cling cling cling.

"It's just the nursery rhyme," I whisper to myself. "Just a song, and a song can't hurt you."

"*It's just the nursery rhyme, April,*" comes a high-pitched voice.

It's coming
>from
>>my
>>>closet.

Goose bumps race across my skin and I sit up straighter. But I am frozen in place, either by fear or dark magic.

"*A song can't hurt you,*" it parrots.

The nursery rhyme in Freddy's room goes quiet.

So quiet I can hear my frantic breathing.

So quiet I can hear the

>>*tap*
>>>*tap*
>>>>*tap*

>>>of footsteps in my closet.

Something coming out from the shadows.

A shadow itself. So tall it touches the ceiling, so dark it seems to suck in darkness.

Pitch-black.

Save for two
>glowing

blue

eyes.

"A song can't hurt you," it growls, its voice so deep it makes my bones rattle.

"But soon, I CAN!"

The clown's last words are a roar. It shakes my windows and rattles the dolls off my dresser.

I scream. I close my eyes.

And then, there is nothing but silence.

Silence, and Freddy's tape, playing its final nursery rhyme.

I open my eyes.

I see:

No clown in the closet.

No dolls dropped to the floor.

Just the dark

and the quiet

and the closed closet door.

Closed?

In Freddy's room, I hear the audiobook whisper, in a singsong voice,

"SLEEP TIGHT, APRIL."

Kyle

I can't sleep.

I'm starving. Dad must have forbidden Mom from sneaking me dinner, because I've been locked in my room all night without anything.

Thankfully, I had some leftover Halloween candy.

I want to convince myself that that's why I'm still awake—too much sugar. But the truth is, I can't sleep because I hurt deeper than just hunger. I want to text Deshaun, but he doesn't know how angry Dad can get. Dad doesn't yell as much when other people are around. But I also don't bring other people around much. Why risk it?

But still, I wish Deshaun were here. I want a friend here. More than anything, I want someone to tell me it's going to be okay. Things will get better.

It makes me think about Andres. And even though I know it's stupid, even though I barely know him, that's enough to make the hurting stop. Just for a little bit. To know there's someone out there who seems, if nothing else, kind.

I slow my breathing. Try to feel heavy, try to turn off my thoughts.

I try to sleep. At least when I wake up, this terrible day will finally be over.

Darkness slithers around me.

I wake slowly, whatever I was dreaming about falling from my brain like a blanket. I'm awake, and my bed is cold. So very cold. The light from the streetlamp outside washes pale white over my bedspread. I turn over and pull the covers tighter, closing my eyes. I think I was dreaming about flying. And magical powers.

Whatever it was, it's definitely better than being awake in my crummy house with my crummy father.

I feel sleep sliding in.

And something
                slithers
        over my fingers.
I jerk my hand back. My heart immediately pounds
in my chest and my eyes snap open. I reach around,
but there's nothing there. Phew. A dream. One of
those strange feelings you get when falling asleep.
There's no way there's a snake in my bed. No way . . .
    I close my eyes again, try to force out the image of
snakes because that's just stupid, it's just my mind
playing tricks. The snakes can't get out of their cages.
And they *definitely* can't make it out of the basement and up two flights of stairs.
    Another cold
            coiling
                something
                    slides over my shins.
I yelp and sit bolt upright.
I throw back my covers.
        Snakes
            swarm
                the foot of my bed.
Black and red and green, poisonous and angry,
they curl and coil over themselves in the pale

streetlamp. They seem to wince back when the light hits them, hissing ominously. But that lasts only a moment. Because now I have revealed them. Now I have revealed myself.

As one, their beady black eyes
all
turn
toward me.

Snakes I've never seen before swarm my bed. Cobras unfold and rise to meet my eyes. Vipers hiss and coil, ready to strike. Anacondas drape over the bed's sides, thick and ready to crush me whole.

Adrenaline shoots through my veins. The only thing I can think is *RUN!*

I leap from my bed.

But rather than hitting the soft carpet of my floor,
my feet
sink
in snakes.

I let out a scream as I topple to the ground. Lightning fast, the snakes are on top of me. Twisting around my thighs, coiling around my neck, heavy and cold, and all I can think of is the grave we dug up, the weight of cold earth on my chest. All I hear is the hissing. The hissing.

I thrash and flail. I yell out, but the snakes wrap over my mouth, cutting off my cries. They tighten. Crushing my chest. Constricting my lungs.

The dark room goes black as snakes cover my eyes. As they squeeze the life out of me—

"What the heck is going on?" my dad roars.

I jolt. The light flips on. Light floods the room.

The empty room.

No snakes.

Just me on the ground, wrapped tight and fighting against my comforter. Just me, and my dad in the doorway, staring down at me like he doesn't understand how he could have such an idiot son.

"I—I . . ." I stammer. I can't even choke out *had a bad dream*. I can't say anything at all.

"Pathetic," Dad growls. "Some people in this house are trying to sleep. Do you understand that?"

He doesn't help me unravel myself. He just flicks off the light and slams the door shut behind him, muttering that if I wake him up again, he'll really give me something to lose sleep over.

I close my eyes and listen to his footfalls fade through the floorboards. I try to slow my breathing, try to calm my frantic heartbeat.

I don't get back up.

I lie there on the ground, still wrapped in the comforter, and wait for morning to come.

Andres

I wake up Sunday morning drenched in sweat, dreams of being lost in the middle of the ocean still haunting me.

My heart races so fast I feel like I've been running.

It takes a few minutes to blink away the dream. To see my bedroom, rather than an endless expanse of churning blue-gray waves.

Unbroken waves.

Unbroken, save for the very end. When a gray fin sliced up toward the sky and raced straight toward me.

Even awake, the thought of that shark fin is

enough to make fresh sweat break out over my skin. I take a deep breath and wipe off my forehead.

I need to shower. But being around water is the last thing I want right now.

Instead, I run to the bathroom and grab a rag and wipe off my sweat that way. It's not as good as a shower, but no. Just no.

I stare at my phone after getting dressed. No messages from April. Or anyone else, for that matter. I want to call her, because we normally hang out on Sundays to do homework and watch bad movies. But I don't. I can't. And I don't know why.

After the bath last night, I sort of feel like I'm losing my mind.

Had she experienced something similar?

Should I apologize for doubting her?

I tell myself I fell asleep in the tub and had a nightmare. And that nightmare stuck to my brain and followed me when I fell asleep. Totally normal. Especially after the graveyard.

If anything, I probably had the bad dream because April had a bad dream, and I was worried about her.

Yeah, that's it.

I tell myself that it's not worth worrying anyone

over, and that April was overreacting yesterday and it's not my place to reach out first. I can see why she got freaked out, yes. But that doesn't give her an excuse to ghost me like that.

I spend the rest of my morning with my family—a breakfast of scrambled eggs and orange juice, a few hours of doing homework at the kitchen table while my brothers run around me like wild men. And before I know it, it's lunch, and I still haven't gotten a text from April or anything. It makes me feel like I've done something wrong.

I decide that there's no way I'm going to spend the rest of the day inside, waiting for my best friend to call. It's nice out, and my brothers are starting to give me a headache. So I grab my coat and head out the door with some of my allowance money jingling in my pocket.

The day is crisp and clear and everything looks so, I don't know, peaceful, that it's hard to believe I had a nightmare last night. It's hard to believe that I woke up covered in sweat, and that just two nights ago I crept through a graveyard and then had my best friend freak out on me. I mean, it's sunny and there are still scarecrows and pumpkins in people's yards, and kids are out jumping in piles of leaves and laughing. It's a very Midwest sort of afternoon, and it makes it impossible to think that anything bad could happen here.

I head toward our one little café at the edge of downtown. There are paper skeletons in the window and toy bats hanging from the ceiling fans, and when I step inside it smells like coffee and spices and burnt cheese. I order a hot chocolate and a panini and go grab a seat at the bar along the window, watching some little kids across the street play tag. They're all in their costumes, even though Halloween is over, and their costumes are all onesies. They remind me of Freddy, which makes me think of April, which makes me want to call her again . . .

"Andres?"

I jolt, thinking maybe it's my order, but it's not. It's Kyle.

He stands nervously in the doorway, like he isn't certain if he wants to come in and order something or run the other way. Just seeing him makes my chest go warm. I pat the stool beside me.

"How's it going?" I ask when he finally sits down.

"Um, okay," he replies.

For a very awkward moment we just sit there, staring at the counter.

"Were you, um, going to get something?" I ask.

He practically jumps in his seat when I talk, like I've surprised him, or he was zoned out and somewhere else entirely.

"Oh yeah," he says distractedly. He heads over to the counter and waits in line to order.

I try not to look at him. He seems about as stressed and tired as I am. Maybe he's having nightmares as well. Should I ask him? I mean, I barely know the guy. That seems weird, right? The waiter comes over and sets down my hot cocoa and sandwich, and I thank him distractedly. Kyle just looks so . . . lost.

I'm so busy not-looking at him that I only see the movement outside the window from the corner of my eye.

A gray fin, just beyond the roof of a car.

I glance over. But no, it's just someone wearing a gray beanie. It's not even pointy. What in the world is wrong with me?

"You okay?" Kyle asks. He sits down with a to-go coffee. Black. He must really not be sleeping well.

"Yeah. Just, um, thought I saw something."

He nods and sips his coffee and I take my cocoa but I don't eat my sandwich. Even though my stomach is grumbling, it feels weird to eat in front of him, and I know it's stupid, but I can't force it away. He looks hungry. And very, very tired.

"How've you been sleeping?" he asks.

I half choke on the cocoa. Hot. Too hot. At least, that's what I tell myself. Kyle doesn't laugh, though. He barely even seems to be in the same room as me.

"Okay," I lie.

"Good," he replies. "Good. Me too. Yeah. Just fine." He looks away again.

"Hey," I say softly. "You okay?"

"Yeah. Just fine," he repeats. He pushes himself up to standing. "I gotta run, though."

"Yeah." He starts heading to the door. "Hey," I call out. He pauses.

"What?"

"Can I get your number?"

I don't know what makes me ask, but with April mad at me and these weird nightmares, I don't know . . . I guess I feel like I should stay in touch with those of us who were in the graveyard Friday night. Well, everyone except for Caroline.

Kyle actually blushes.

"Sure," he says, and steps over to type it in my phone.

"Thanks," I say. "Oh, um, hey. Do you want this?"

I hold out half of my panini.

"Oh no, I'm fine. Thanks."

"No, it's okay. I'm not going to eat it and I feel bad trashing it."

He looks at the sandwich. I swear I hear his stomach rumble. I pretend not to hear it.

"I guess . . . if you insist."

"I do." This is easily the most awkward conversation I've ever had, but I hand over the panini and he takes a bite. And smiles.

"Thank you," he says.

"Of course. Catch you later."

He nods and heads toward the door.

Despite everything, when I watch him walk away, I realize I am smiling too.

Kyle

I shouldn't have given Andres my number.

I shouldn't be talking to anyone right now.

I feel like I'm losing my mind, and the fewer people I talk to, the fewer chances anyone has of finding out about it.

I don't really know where I'm going. I'd hoped to spend the afternoon at the café, maybe reading, maybe just staring out the window, but with Andres there, there's no way I can just hang. I'd say something. He'd ask something. And then he'd learn that I've been hallucinating things and, I don't know, never want to talk to me again.

A part of me wants to text Deshaun, but I can't risk that either. He knows me too well.

"Stupid," I hiss to myself, when my phone buzzes. Andres. Just sending me his number.

I shouldn't have asked him how he was sleeping. I'm too tired. I need to, I don't know, go take a nap somewhere. Somewhere I won't find anyone. Not Andres. Not Deshaun. Especially not my dad.

I don't even realize where I'm heading until my feet crunch on the dry leaves.

I halt. My blood goes cold.

Somehow, without even thinking about it, I've ended up at the graveyard.

"No," I whisper.

Clouds have somehow covered the sky, making everything cold and gray. From here, I can't see anyone else amid the graves. Just me. Why did I come here? Of all places, why here?

"What are you doing here?"

I nearly jump out of my skin.

It's April.

I try to gather my wits, but it's hard. My brain is barely functioning right now.

"I could ask you the same," I reply. Smooth.

She shrugs. Not like she's brushing off the statement, but like she's uncomfortable. Like she doesn't want to be here either.

"I don't know," she finally admits. "I just . . . showed up, I guess."

"That doesn't make any sense," I reply.

"And you never answered."

I take a sip of my coffee. It's already gone cold. I finished the panini a block ago.

"Same, I guess. Just didn't want to be home."

"Same."

We stand there in silence for a few moments. No one drives past on the road behind us. No one drives through the cemetery. It honestly feels like she and I are the only ones in the whole world right now.

It honestly feels like the whole world has ceased to exist.

Just the graveyard, pulling us forward for reasons I can't explain.

I look over to her. Really look. There are dark circles under her eyes, and her tan skin is pale. She looks like she has a cold. Just like me. Just like Andres. Just like Deshaun.

What in the world is going on?

"Why did you come out Friday night?" she asks. "You didn't get a note, right?"

I shake my head.

"No. I guess I just wanted to make sure Deshaun was okay. He's . . . not having the best time with high school. Figured if kids were pulling a prank on him, I wanted to have his back, you know?"

She nods, but doesn't take her eyes off the graves.

"You didn't need to be a part of this," she whispers to herself.

"What?"

"Oh, um . . ." She shakes her head and looks at me.

My phone buzzes. Andres again. Asking if I want to grab coffee after school tomorrow.

April glances over at my phone.

"You have his number?" she asks.

"Yeah," I reply. I shove my phone back in my pocket. My fingers brush against a piece of paper. Probably my receipt from the café. "Ran into him a little bit ago. Why?"

The way she looks makes me feel like I've done something wrong.

"Nothing," she says.

"Seems like something."

"It's nothing. We just aren't talking right now, okay?"

"Does it have to do with the graveyard?" I ask. I don't know why I ask it.

"Have you been having nightmares?" she demands, her voice unusually shrill.

"No," I say immediately. "Why?"

The look she gives me makes me wish I hadn't lied. She looks like she's lost in the middle of the sea.

"It's nothing," she says once more. She burrows deeper in her coat. "I'm going home. Too cold. Enjoy the tombstones."

I watch her go.

I should call out to her. Tell her I was lying about not having nightmares. Tell her that I didn't just come to the graveyard because of Deshaun. That I felt a pull. That I knew it was where I was supposed to be.

I don't say a thing.

I clench my phone. It buzzes again. *Andres.*

Then there's another sensation. Something moving across my knuckles. Something is *in my pocket, and that something is alive!*

I yelp.

Yank out my hand.

And out coils a snake.

Long and thin and banded with green, like a great, cold spaghetti noodle. It drops to the ground and I leap back. I swear it raises its head and looks at me. Like it knows I'm afraid. Like it knows it doesn't belong.

Then it sinuously slides into the grass, leaving behind something that at first I think must be the receipt from the café.

Only it's not.

It's a note.

Written on the same orange paper as the one Deshaun received. And I know it wasn't in my pocket this morning.

I stare at it for a long while.

And once I'm certain that the snake is long gone, I bend over and pick up the note with trembling hands.

Written on the other side in black paint are the words:

I knew you'd come to the graveyard. You can't escape the fear you live with and you'll never escape me.

April

Freddy and Mom must still be out running errands or something, because the house is completely empty when I get there. Completely empty, and completely cold.

I know my mom keeps the heat low during the autumn months because she doesn't want to rack up the electricity bills, but this feels colder than usual. Colder than outside. The moment I walk into the house, I feel like I'm stepping into a refrigerator.

A very dark, very quiet refrigerator.

Suddenly, I think that maybe coming back home was a mistake. Even if staying out in the graveyard with Kyle was frustrating, at least there I had someone else to keep me safe. Maybe I should call Andres . . .

"Get ahold of yourself," I whisper. "It's the middle of the day and you are *not* calling Andres because you're scared of your own house."

Admittedly, saying that out loud makes me feel a little better. Not much, but a little. I may not know what's going on, but I'm not going to let it make me scared of my own home. Just as I'm not going to let myself become so scared and weak that I call Andres to keep me company. I'm still angry with him, and I'm not going to stop until he apologizes. Or says that he truly believes me.

I go into the kitchen and grab a glass of orange juice when I hear it.

A squeak.

A footstep.

Right above my head. Which means . . .

It's coming
    from
        my
            room.

I freeze.

Strain my ears.

Maybe I was just hearing things. Maybe it was just the house creaking. It's an old house. Old houses do that sometimes.

CREAK.

I drop the glass. It falls to the counter and shatters, spilling orange juice all over.

What do I do?

I reach for my phone. Should I call Mom? Should I call Andres? The cops?

There is someone in my house.

In *my room*!

"April?"

My fear drops in a moment. I know that voice.

"Freddy?" I call out.

What is Freddy doing home without Mom? And what is he doing in my room?

I look at the spilled orange juice and broken glass. I should clean it up before Mom comes down or Freddy gets hurt. Then Freddy calls out again.

"April, where are you?"

"Down here, buddy!" I call out.

"April?"

He sounds scared. Maybe he hurt himself playing?

"Coming, buddy!" I say.

I run up the stairs, partially wondering where Mom is and partially wondering what has Freddy so scared. When I reach my room, those thoughts drop from my mind.

Freddy isn't in here.

"Freddy?" I call out.

I stand in my doorway and look around. At my unmade bed. At the pile of blankets Andres slept in the other night. At the closed closet door.

Wait.

I thought I'd opened that before leaving. Just to make sure there wasn't anything lingering inside. Just because, in the light of day, it didn't seem as scary. Now I stare at the door and fear hammers in my chest.

It could be hiding anything.

"Freddy?" I ask again, much quieter this time.

No answer.

Suddenly, I'm reminded of just how quiet the house is. Just how cold. Shivers race over my skin.

I step toward the closet.

Reach out a hand.

"Freddy?" I whisper. My voice squeaks.

I grab the doorknob and twist. My heart thuds so loudly I don't even hear it squeak open.

What I see makes my heart stop.

The closet is empty.

No clown.

No Freddy.

No one at all.

No one. Just a tiny tin box sitting open on the floor, a scrap of paper inside with two bold words written on it.

I'M HERE

Deshaun

My room looks like some sort of supernatural battle-field, but not one part of me thinks it's going to keep the ghost away.

I went to the library as soon as it opened and spent hours looking through books, trying to find something—*anything* that could help me. But most of the books on magic were recent and only had stupid love spells and charms that were so cheesy there was no way they would actually work. I needed something serious. Something tried and tested. These were definitely just fluff.

The movies and stories all lied. In stories, the haunted kid always finds the answers he needs in the library. That's where all the answers in the world are, right? So what does it mean that I couldn't find anything? What was I supposed to do? Try to find something online? Please. I'd have better luck finding something serious in a book on "easy charms for the serious homemaker."

Instead, I turned to my other books. The fantasies and supernatural thrillers. They, at least, provided *some* sort of insight into how to fend off ghosts.

Now, with darkness closing in, it doesn't seem like it's enough.

I stand at the edge of my room and survey my work.

The circle of salt clearly didn't work, so I ran to a local touristy shop and grabbed a bunch of cheap quartz crystal pieces. They ring my bed, along with a line of Himalayan pink salt that was double the price of normal table salt and better be worth it. I also have little note cards scribbled with runes and magical symbols, as well as protective images from everything I could think of. Crosses and Stars of David and pentacles and hamsas. There are votive candles to saints and angels at the four corners of my room. More crystals and salt lining the base of my windows and doors. Pages and pages of mantras and protective charms for me to recite (because okay, yes, I did print some stuff from online). A Bible under my pillow. A wooden stake on top of my headboard. Even some holy water in a small dish on my nightstand, which I grabbed from the oldest church in town I could find. (I wanted to ask the priest if he knew how to fight off ghosts, but, again, I've seen the movies—adults never trust kids when they say they're fighting evil.)

And yet, even with everything I can think of protecting me, it doesn't seem like enough.

I want to invite Kyle over. But even though I've reached out a few times, he said he was busy, and besides, tonight is a school night, and even though my parents love him, there's no way they'd let him stay over when I have school the next morning.

That, and I have no doubt that he would laugh at me. Even *I* think this looks ridiculous, and I'm depending on it to save my life.

I hear my parents call out that it's dinnertime.

I give my room one last look and close the door, locking it behind me with a skeleton key.

Kyle

I don't know what I dread more—heading to dinner or going to bed after. I've tried to avoid home all day, but there's no more putting it off. I know that my dad will be home. And I know that it won't be a happy dinner. Just like the rest of them.

Mom is leaning against the kitchen counter when I get in, a glass of wine in hand, and she stares nervously at the man sitting at our dining room table. I know that look. He's been drinking all day.

Dad barely looks up from his pasta when I come in. I see he's taken most of the garlic bread as well. There are three bottles of beer on the table beside his heaping plate, and only one of them is full. Even that is only half.

Mom nods to the meal with a nervous smile. The table is set with spaghetti and sauce, garlic bread, and bagged salad. An attempt at a wholesome family meal. My mind races. I'm in no mood to pretend to be a family tonight.

I load up my plate silently. She sits down and starts doing the same.

I don't sit down.

"I have a lot of homework to do," I lie. "I think I'll eat in my room and work—"

"You sit down!" Dad roars. He slams his fist on the table, making plates and silverware shake. Then he stares straight at me, his eyes narrowed and angry. Like always. "Your mother made you a meal, and you will *not* disrespect her by leaving."

My mouth goes sour. I want to throw a chair at him, to tell him that he is no person to speak about respect. I don't give in to my anger, though. I don't throw a chair or yell back. I swallow all of my pride and look to my mom, who stares at me with apologies and fear laced through her expression. I know she's torn. Just as I know she'll never speak out against my father. She's too afraid.

The entire room is still. Tense. Waiting for me to decide what to do.

I sit down at the table across from my father.

The tension cuts. I practically hear my mom sigh. But it's not like we suddenly become a happy family— Dad goes back to eating his pasta silently, barely looking at me, but when he does, it's with venom in his eyes.

And then I hear it.

At first, I think it's the sink running.

A low, slinking hiss.

It takes a moment for me to realize the rest of the world has gone silent.

I glance up.

Mom is paused with her fork halfway to her mouth. Not blinking. Not moving. Staring at Dad, who also doesn't move a muscle.

What in the world?

The hissing grows louder, and I realize it's coming not from the faucet, but from Dad. He hunches over his plate, his eyes looking down at the half-eaten

pasta, his fork twined with noodles. His mouth is
slightly open.

And that's where the hissing comes from.

"Dad?" I whisper. "What—?"

Something moves in his mouth.

I think it's his tongue.

It stretches.

        Not his tongue.

The head of a snake.

    It drips down from his lips,
        stretching
          twisting
            slinking
              down toward the plate
            where it flops
        and coils
      rearing its head up to stare
           straight
          at
                me
                just
         as
      another snake

                    slides
                              from Dad's lips.

The first snake hisses.

Tenses.

Opens its mouth wide, revealing razor-sharp teeth.

The snake strikes.

I jerk back to standing, knocking my chair to the ground with a crash.

"Kyle, what the heck?" Dad roars.

And just like that, the kitchen is back to normal. Dad sits there with his fork raised to his mouth; Mom stares at me with wide eyes.

No snakes anywhere.

No snakes.

I swallow and pick up my chair.

"Sorry," I say, but I don't know who I'm apologizing to. "I, um, I just . . ."

Dad is laughing, though, calling me an idiot and a hundred other names under his breath.

I don't bother finishing the rest of the sentence, or my dinner. I mumble that I'm feeling sick and leave.

When I reach my bedroom, I close the door behind me and curl up on my bed, rocking back and forth and holding myself back from reaching out to Deshaun or Andres or April, the only people in this entire world who might actually understand.

I can't risk leaving.

And I can't risk them coming here.

Not with the snakes around. Not with my dad.

Deshaun

I don't head back up to my bedroom until it's time to go to sleep. I spend the night watching TV with my parents. They try to ask me about school and all that, but I can barely focus on what they're saying. I can barely keep my eyes open. All I can think about is how tired I am, and whether or not my magical protective force field will be enough to keep the poltergeist at bay. Finally, when I can't stop yawning, Dad gently forces me to go brush my teeth and go to bed.

I trudge upstairs and head into my room to change into pj's.

I unlock the door.

And freeze.

Blink.

Rub my eyes.

But no, I'm not imagining things.

Everything I bought today, everything I made, all of it . . .

        is on

           my

              ceiling.

A ring of salt circles my ceiling fan.

Pages of symbols plaster its perimeter.

My sci-fi book is open in the center, dripping water.

Even the candles are upside down in the four corners.

No way.

There is no.

           Possible.

              Way.

"Deshaun?" my dad calls from behind me.

I gasp.

As one, everything on the ceiling falls to the ground, a great, resounding clatter of breaking glass and crystal.

Dad runs the rest of the way toward me. He pushes

153

the door open all the way to survey the mess of my room.

"What did you do?" he asks, shocked.

I can't say anything. I just stand there, looking at the ruins of my best attempt at saving myself, and wonder if I've just made things a thousand percent worse.

April

I don't sleep.

When dawn finally breaks Monday morning, my head hurts and my eyes are dry and it feels like my body has been run over by a truck. A couple of times.

I tried sleeping. Really. I read a book cover to cover in the hopes it would knock me out. I watched five episodes of my favorite anime. I put on quiet music. Anything I could think of to make myself fall asleep.

And my body tried to sleep.

The trouble was, every single time I started to drift, I heard it.

The sound of jingling bells in my closet.

The telltale giggle of the clown.

Every time, I'd bolt upright, wide-awake, and check out the closet.

Nothing was there.

Nothing was ever there.

That's a lie. I fell asleep once. Just for a bit.

I'd closed my eyes and felt myself drift and this time, rather than hearing the bells, I'd started to dream. I dreamed that I was six years old again. Back at my birthday party. I stood in the backyard in front of all of my friends, and the clown my parents had brought was doing magic tricks. The clown made me nervous, with its big smile and blue eyes and giant shoes. But he made the kids laugh, and I knew I was supposed to be having fun, and that he was safe, so I let him bring me up front to help him with the trick.

It involved a pie. He said he would make the pie float.

Instead, he tossed the pie in my face.

As I wiped off the cream, everyone in the backyard started to laugh. Started to call me names. Even the clown.

Even though it was my birthday, they made fun of me.

I ran into the house and closed myself in my room and didn't come out. Not until everyone went home and my mom came up and apologized and said the mean clown was gone.

But I could still hear his giggling. Still hear the sound of the bells jingling on his shoes.

The same jingling I heard from my closet.

The same giggling from the graveyard.

When I woke from the dream, only five minutes had passed, but I heard the clown's distant laughter all the same.

By the time the sun rises and I smell the coffee coming from downstairs, I really wonder if I'm losing my mind.

I check my phone while I'm eating breakfast. Andres has been trying to get in touch, saying we need to meet up before school. Tacked on to the very end of the message are six words:

I'm so, so sorry. I understand.

I respond immediately and head out the door to meet at the park a block from the school. We have forty minutes before school starts—it's not a lot of time, but it's enough.

Surprisingly, Andres is already at the park when I arrive.

Even more surprisingly, he's not alone.

"What are you guys doing here?" I ask.

Kyle and Deshaun stand with guarded expressions on their faces. Both of them have their hands in their pockets and shoulders by their ears, like they're freezing cold. But it's a nice, cool autumn day. It's then that I realize their eyes are red. All of them.

"Andres said you had a nightmare," Deshaun says tentatively. "The night we went to the graveyard."

I glare at Andres, but he only shrugs. He doesn't know that the nightmare was just the beginning.

"I did too," Andres adds quickly. He gulps. "Only it didn't seem like a nightmare. Saturday night. I fell asleep in the tub and I . . . I . . ." He cuts off. "You'll laugh."

No one says anything. The air between us is heavy and powerful and expectant. It's clear none of us are going to laugh.

"There was a shark. In my tub." He says it quickly and quietly, like he doesn't want to admit it aloud. "I thought it was going to eat me." He looks down at his feet, then up at me. His face goes pale. "It sounds stupid, but . . . I *felt* it. It was real. I know it was. Last night I had another nightmare. This one was much worse."

"I had it happen too," Deshaun says. "My computer turned on Friday night. And it . . . it showed all of us in the graveyard. Digging something out of the grave. And whatever it was took over the whole screen. Like some sort of ghost. Or demon. And last night I tried to protect myself—and whatever is haunting me put every single protection charm I made on the ceiling, before letting them drop and destroy my room."

"What about you?" I ask Kyle. "Did you see anything?"

"Not the first night," Kyle says. "But Saturday night. There were snakes in my bed. Real snakes. They tried to choke me." His voice lowers. "Then yesterday . . . there were snakes in my pocket. And when I yanked out my hand, there was this."

He hands over a note—

Written in the same handwriting as the notes that started all of this for me.

I shiver when I read the words.

You'll never escape me.

I hand the note back to him. He doesn't look like he wants to take it.

A dozen different emotions war within me.

They've all had something scary happen to them. They believe me. I'm not alone. But also . . .

"So this is real," I whisper. "Really real."

Deshaun nods. "When Kyle texted me this morning, I honestly thought I was going insane. I didn't sleep at all last night. I thought I was the only one."

"You're not," I say. "I couldn't sleep either."

Kyle keeps looking down at his shoes. Andres looks over at him; I know that look. Andres wants to comfort Kyle, but he doesn't know how. I don't really either. All I know is, we're all in this together.

"So we all saw *something*," I say. "I mean, everyone who was in the graveyard is having nightmares."

"Not everyone," Andres says.

I glance at him. I know who he's talking about, but it still makes me angry that he'd reach out to her.

"I, uh, messaged Caroline," he continues. "Asked her how she was doing. How she was sleeping. She told me not to talk to her."

Just her name makes me angry, and hearing that she's sleeping fine while the rest of us are having night-mares, when all of this really is her fault, makes me even angrier. If anyone deserves to be losing sleep, it's her.

"Then it's just us four," Deshaun says. He pauses. "What do we do?"

I shrug uncomfortably. It's the question I've been asking myself all weekend.

"What *is* there to do?" Kyle asks. He looks to his friend. "I mean, they're just stupid nightmares, right? Bad dreams can't hurt us."

"But sleep deprivation can," Andres pipes in. "They've done studies. You can only last, like, eleven days."

"Before?" I ask.

He doesn't answer. At least, not that part of the question.

"After a few days, you start to hallucinate," he says, as if he didn't hear me.

"I'd say we're already hallucinating," Kyle says. His voice is bitter.

"It's not hallucinations," Andres says. "Halluci-nations can't make notes show up in your pocket, or levitate half your room."

"So what is it?" Kyle asks. He almost sounds angry.

"I think we're being haunted," Deshaun says quietly.

"This is ridiculous," Kyle says. "We fell prey to some stupid prank in the graveyard and let our imaginations get away from us. That's it."

"If you believe that, why did you come here?" I ask. "How do you explain that note?"

He doesn't answer.

"Look," I continue. "I get it; I don't want to believe it either. But I *know* I'm not hallucinating or making things up. Something is following us. And if I'm right, I think I know what it's doing."

When Andres looks at me, he actually seems excited for the first time in our entire conversation.

"What?"

"Well," I tell him. "I *hate* clowns. More than anything. And that's what I saw in my closet. Andres, you're scared of sharks. So you dreamed you saw that in your bathtub." Andres blushes, but he doesn't argue. "Deshaun, I'm guessing you're scared of—"

"Ghosts," he replies. "Poltergeists, mainly. You know, ghosts that move or haunt objects. Remember that story about the kid who got lost in the graveyard?"

I nod.

"Yeah, that was me."

Kyle gapes.

"Really? You never told me."

"I was embarrassed," Deshaun says. "Besides, there never seemed like a good time to mention it. And even if I had, you wouldn't have believed me."

"Believed that you got lost?"

Deshaun shakes his head. "No," he says quietly. "Not lost. I was trapped. And I . . . I saw things that night. Ghosts. Demons. I don't know. They whispered terrible things and wailed all night long. As I got older, I thought maybe I'd made it up. Now I'm not so sure."

I swallow. I want to reach out and take his hand but I don't know him well enough. Kyle pats him on the shoulder comfortingly. I'm about to ask Kyle what he's scared of, but after Deshaun's admission, I don't think we need to talk about fears anymore.

I go on. "Don't you get it? Whatever this is, it's showing us our deepest, darkest fears! That's why we all see something different."

"So how do we stop it?" Andres asks. "Whatever this thing is."

Kyle keeps shaking his head.

"This is ridiculous," he says. "There isn't some sort of ghost haunting us! Face reality, guys. There are much scarier things than whatever we're making up in our heads."

"Dude—" Deshaun begins, but Kyle cuts him off.

"No, I'm not standing around here freezing my butt off any longer. You guys want to fight ghosts, fine. But I'm going to stay rooted in reality. This is just stupid. Someone is messing with us, giving us bad dreams. Bad dreams can't hurt us. Period."

He turns to begin walking away.

He takes a few steps.

And then, I hear it.

The jingle of bells.

The high-pitched laughter.

Kyle freezes. We all do.

Because there, standing beside the swing set, is the clown from my nightmare. He waves at the four of us, his mouth so wide it seems to be splitting his face, his teeth sharp as needles and eyes blue ice.

Then he points at us, one at a time, and his smile stretches impossibly wider.

A gust of wind billows leaves and dust around us, making me blink.

The clown is gone.

PART THREE
the clown

Kyle

The moment I see the clown, I know this is no hallucination.

I still desperately want that to be the case. Want to believe someone just left the note in my pocket, and the snake just, I don't know, crawled in or something. But that clown . . . that clown sends a chill so deep in my heart that I know none of us are making any of this up.

It stares at me, and its smile seems meant for me alone.

I swear it *does* know my deepest, darkest fears. And that smile tells me that it will do everything it can to bring them about.

I swear it has my father's eyes.

"Did you see that?" Deshaun yelps the moment the clown vanishes. "Did everyone see that?"

I can only nod, and I hear the others behind me mumble their terrified agreement. We've all seen the clown.

"Where did it go?" Andres whispers.

"It knows," April replies. Her voice quivers with fear. "It knows that we've been talking about it. It knows we've caught on."

"So?" I say. I try to push down my own fear, try to melt the ice that seems to freeze my bones in place. I turn and face them. "Even if it knows that we've been talking—so what? I mean, it hasn't actually hurt any of us, right? It's just scaring us. I mean, has anyone been physically hurt?"

We all shake our heads.

"So far," April mutters.

"I say we all have a sleepover," Andres says. "That way none of us are alone. We've all watched scary movies before, right? Our powers combined, I'm sure we can try to figure out how to stop it."

Everyone seems on board for this monster-hunting

party. They don't seem to understand that for some of us, the monster already lives in our house.

"Where can we stay?" Deshaun asks. "I could ask my parents, but I don't think they'd ever let me have a girl stay over." He blushes and looks at April. I know that look. Deshaun is crushing on her. "Sorry. They're old-fashioned."

She shrugs. "We could stay at mine."

"On a school night?" Deshaun pushes.

"Sure, we have big enough sofas that you two could sleep on. Andres stays over all the time."

"I can't," I say immediately.

"Why not?" April asks. "I can have my mom call your parents and—"

"I just can't, okay? My parents would never allow it. I'm grounded."

"This seems bigger than being grounded," Andres begins, but it's Deshaun who cuts him off.

"Nah. You don't want to push this one. Kyle's parents never budge on punishment."

I look at him. There's a part of me that wants to thank him for stepping in so I don't have to explain myself. The rest hates that it's even necessary.

"I'll be fine," I say. "Promise. It's just bad dreams and visions, right? I can handle another night of snakes."

The three of them nod. They seem uncertain.

Trouble is, so am I.

Deshaun

I'm worried. Not just because we've all seen some sort of phantom clown, and not just because we're all apparently being haunted and given nightmares of our deepest fears.

I'm worried because Kyle looks terrible—his skin is even more pallid than usual and his eyes are so tired they look bruised. There's only one thing in the world that makes Kyle look like that. And it's not ghosts or snakes or nightmares.

It's his dad.

He thinks I don't know that his dad is terrible. He thinks I don't worry. But I do.

I wish I could figure out what was most important—figuring out how to save all of us from a phantom, or trying to figure out how to get Kyle's dad out of his life for good.

"Maybe there's a clue in the graveyard," I say, even though just thinking about the graveyard makes me sick. Every time we mention it, I'm reminded of being lost in there. Reminded of the phantoms that stalked me, that imprisoned me until sunrise.

I thought I had escaped. Now I'm starting to think differently.

April shakes her head. "I was there yesterday. There wasn't anything."

"Come on," I say. I have to feel like we're doing something. I can't imagine just waiting around all day for night to fall. We have to find an answer to end this. Soon. "Let's go check again. We have a little time before school starts. Maybe we'll find something with the four of us."

"I don't know . . ." April says.

"It's okay," Andres tells her. He takes her arm consolingly. "It's morning. Nothing bad can happen now, right?"

"Are you all forgetting that clown?" Kyle asks dryly. He seems to realize he's being a jerk when he says it, because he immediately lowers his eyes again.

"No," April whispers. "I'll never forget that. Ever."

We head to the graveyard together. The late autumn sun is tilting above the trees and the sky is clear blue, but there's a chill that whispers of winter on our heels. A promise of cold that none of us can shake. And it's not just the wind or weather that makes me shiver.

With every footstep toward the graveyard, the sensation of being followed grows stronger.

I keep glancing around as we walk through downtown. Staring at kids and adults with the same sense of trepidation.

It doesn't help that everyone we pass seems to be watching us.

We stay close together as we walk. No one says anything. No one tries to make a joke. We keep our heads down and walk past the old Halloween decorations, the costumed mannequins and plastic bats and leering pumpkins, the gaggles of kids on their way to class, and we try to pretend that we aren't there.

I swear I feel eyes on the back of my neck. Someone is definitely watching me.

I glance over. A kid is walking past, wearing a winter coat with the burgundy hood pulled up.

I can't see their face.

Not at first.

But they must notice me staring. Because a second later, they turn their head.

Ever

    So

      Slowly

And the clown stares back.

I trip and nearly knock April over. She grabs me just in time to keep me standing.

"Did you—" I gasp. "Did you—"

"What?" she asks. Immediately, everyone jerks to attention, scanning the street wildly.

I look back to the kid.

But now it's just a little girl with black pigtails,

surrounded by her laughing friends. Not a terrifying clown out to get us.

"Nothing," I say. I try to shake it off. "Just imagining things."

I can tell from their expressions that none of them believe it.

April

I'm on high alert the entire walk to the graveyard.

I keep jerking my head to watch people as they pass. Keep jumping when my reflection appears in a storefront window.

I feel like I'm being watched.

It's the same feeling I got Friday night. The same chills when I knew there was something in my closet.

Even here, in the light of day, we. Are. Not. Safe. And I know that the very last place we should be going is the grave that brought all of this about in the first place.

It doesn't help that I know Deshaun saw something.

Even though he's trying to brush it off, I know that look. He's terrified. He's as terrified as I was when the clown first appeared.

At least now they all see it. At least now we all know that we're in this together. The trouble is, I can't tell if that actually changes everything.

Andres takes my arm as we walk through town and up to the graveyard.

"I'm sorry for not believing you earlier," he whispers.

I squeeze his hand. "It's okay, I understand."

I'd expected to be angry with him, but it's impossible to feel anything but relief that things between us are repaired. Like we said—we need to stick together. Now more than ever.

We reach the graveyard and head straight toward the grave. I feel like I could make my way there with my eyes closed at this point. I feel like the graveyard has become a part of me, or I've become a part of *it*, and I'll never be able to get far enough away.

The thought is far from comforting.

The grave is exactly as it was when I last visited—nothing written or carved on the tombstone, and no sign that anyone has been here digging in the last decade. The grass is green and littered with dead leaves, and the gnarled tree beside it reveals nothing, not even pigeons.

"Come on," I say anxiously. I check my phone. We don't have much time. "Let's look. There has to be something around here. *Has* to."

We break up and search around. Kyle inspects the tree, and Deshaun and Andres walk down the hill a bit to see if there's anything nearby.

I drop to my knees and brush aside the leaves.

That's when I see it.

A sock.

Hidden under a pile of leaves at the base of the tombstone.

Not just any sock.

One of *my* socks. Pink with tiny pandas all over it. I wore this the other day. It had been in my hamper.

In my closet.

"Guys," I whisper. Barely a whisper. And yet, they're all at my side in a heartbeat.

"What is it?" Kyle asks.

"My sock."

"What's it doing out here?"

I reach over and pick it up with trembling hands.

"There's something inside," I say.

I don't want to reach inside. Not at all.

Andres must be able to sense my hesitation, because he kneels down beside me and takes it gently. Then he reaches into the sock and pulls out a folded note. When he reads it, his eyes widen with fear.

"What does it say?" Kyle asks.

Andres can't answer. He holds the note out for all of us to see.

one by one, we've had some fun
but none of you five
will come out alive

Andres

We stare at the note for what feels like an hour. No sound, no words between us, not even birds calling out in the cold air. We stare at the note, and the threat feels even more real than before, even more real than seeing the clown gesture at all of us.

This thing doesn't just want to scare us.

It wants to hurt us.

And maybe it can only do that at night, but that's only a few hours away, and we're not even certain that's the case anymore. And we have school until then.

The absolute last thing I want to do is go.

That's the first rule of scary movies, right? Never

split up. And what is school if not a systemized way of splitting kids up?

Deshaun's watch beeps.

"Yikes," he says, silencing the alarm. "We gotta go."

"Maybe we should skip," April says.

"And do what?" Kyle asks. "My dad—my *parents* would kill me if I played hooky."

"Same," Deshaun says. "Besides . . . I spent all day in the library researching yesterday. I didn't learn anything on how to defeat something like this. Everything I tried clearly didn't work."

We go silent. The truth is heavy between us: None of us know how to defeat something like this. We're just normal kids. We aren't equipped to fight ghosts or ultimate evil. It's just us four against something we can't even comprehend.

Wait . . .

"It says five," I say.

"What?" Kyle asks.

"The note. It says *none of you five*. That means—"

"Caroline was lying," April completes. "Of course she was. That's just like her. She *must* be having nightmares too."

"We have to find her," I say.

April crosses her arms over her chest. "We could just let her suffer."

"But maybe she holds the clue," I argue. "I swear she picked something up in the graveyard. She took the tin box away, remember? Maybe there was something inside. A clue we're missing."

"Then you guys will have to find out," Kyle says.

I groan. I forgot that they are at the high school.

"Okay. April, you and Caroline are just going to have to set aside your grudge. We need each other to survive this. All of us." I look to Kyle and Deshaun when I say it. They nod.

"We should go," Deshaun says. "We all have each other's numbers now. We can update throughout the day and meet after school."

"Provided nothing happens," Kyle says.

"Yes," Deshaun says. "That."

He pauses. Then his eyes light up.

"Wait, I have an idea. In movies, right. The protagonists always have to just face their fears to banish the monster. What if that's what we have to do?"

"You want me to face a shark trying to eat me?" I ask. Just the thought makes me shudder.

"No. Well, I mean, yes? Maybe?"

"You don't seem very certain," April says.

"I'm not! But it's our best shot. Maybe if we start facing our fears, they'll go away." He seems to lose conviction and stares down at his feet. "I mean, it's worth a try. It's not like we have any better ideas."

I nod. I don't like this plan, don't like that we're going to split up for eight hours, but it's the only thing we can do. And it's not like he's asking me to track down a shark and throw myself into its tank. Or at least I don't think that's what he's asking me. Because if I have to swim with an actual shark . . . I'm not sure the whole *face your fears* thing is going to work.

"Nothing bad will happen," I say. "We just have to stick together." I glance at April. "Easy, right?"

She doesn't respond. None of them do.

Caroline

I walk to school with tears drying behind my eyes.

When I step into the main hall, I don't see any other kids.

I only see the tunnel.

The walls of dirt.

They surround me.

Every step, and they close another inch.

Suffocating me.

Burying me.

April

I can't believe Andres wants us to talk to Caroline. It's bad enough that she was involved at the beginning, but now she has to be a part of it again?

Neither he nor I talks the entire way to school. What is there to talk about? Homework doesn't seem important when a deadly clown is chasing us. Worrying about a test doesn't compare to worrying about how we're going to face our fears.

Because my fear is the clown himself. How in the world am I supposed to face *that*?

It's strange, stepping into the school. It's so normal. Like, shouldn't there be creepy music or flickering lights going on in the background? Something to show that everything has changed and nothing will ever be safe again? But no—kids are laughing and shoving each other and playing music, and Andres and I walk through them all, heads down, terrified at what we'll see if we look someone in the eye.

It makes me wish Deshaun was here. I mean, Andres makes me feel safe, sure. But Deshaun, well . . . he's *older*. He knows all about this sort of stuff, and that makes me think he knows how to tackle it.

And he's cute.

I push the thought down with a blush. This is *no* time to be thinking about that. He probably wouldn't even be interested, anyway.

"Where's Caroline?" I ask when we pass her locker. She isn't there. And neither are her two annoying friends.

Andres glances around. "No clue. Maybe we try finding her at lunch?"

I nod.

We stand there, unmoving. We have two minutes to get to class, and neither of us wants to be the one to break away. Because that will mean we are separated for the next three hours. Maybe we'll pass by each other in the hall. But without him around, I feel . . .

"I'm so scared," he whispers.

"Me too," I admit. I keep glancing around. Expecting kids to be staring at us suspiciously or something. No one does.

I go on. "But I mean . . . you should be fine, right? It's not like you're taking classes in the ocean or something. Unless you're worried about flying sharks."

Andres's eyes go wide as I talk. His mouth drops open.

"What?" I ask.

"It's Monday," he whispers.

"Yeah. So?"

"So Monday we're starting swimming in gym class."

My breath catches in my throat. I try to push it down and appear strong for him, though, because the last thing he needs is to see me looking worried.

"I'm sure it will be okay," I say. I take his arm consolingly. It clearly doesn't work. "Just keep reminding yourself that there's no possible way for a shark to get inside a swimming pool. Even if they did, they'd die from the chlorine! And if that doesn't do it, you could always say you're sick."

His face *does* look a little green.

"Yeah," he says distractedly. "Yeah, maybe I'll try that."

The bell rings.

"Okay," he says. "Okay. Um. You stay safe. I'll talk to you soon."

"Yeah," I reply.

He turns and begins walking away, down the hall, his shoulders slumped and head down like a doomed man.

I only watch him go for a second. Then I dash to my locker and store my things. Thankfully, there are no notes from a killer clown in there. One thing is going right today.

As I'm rushing to my first class of the day, I pass by a classroom door.

Two steps past it and I halt.

I peer back slowly, the entire world fading away to a blur of shadows and dull noise.

There, in the window, waving with his maniacal grin, is the clown.

I stare at him, and he stares back, those two pale blue eyes making my entire body run cold.

He's here.

He's *here*.

I can't move. Can't scream.

And then, someone bumps into me, and the world clatters back.

No clown in the door. Just kids racing to make first period.

I swallow the bile in my throat and turn away, hustling to my class.

Even though I can't see him, I feel his eyes on my back every step of the way.

Kyle

"Do you think they're going to be okay?" Deshaun asks after first period. We haven't heard anything from either of them. The way he keeps checking his phone has me thinking the worst.

"They should be," I reply. "They're smart."

I close my locker and start walking toward our next class. Chemistry. So fun. At least we take it together.

"Yeah, but what if something happens to them?" he asks. He checks his phone for what is probably the hundredth time since we got here. I don't check mine. I don't want it to seem like I'm just waiting to hear from Andres. Even though I *am* worried about him. A little.

At least he doesn't have to worry about sharks attacking during English class.

"They're in school," I say. "Think about it—this is, like, the safest place for us to be in a situation like this. We're surrounded by other kids and adults. That *thing* would be stupid to try to attack us now."

"I know, but . . ." He takes a deep breath. "I don't think this is something we can stop or predict."

"You said we should try facing it if we saw it again," I say, raising an eyebrow. "You sounded pretty sure about it."

"I am. I mean, I was. But last night. You don't understand, Kyle. I put out *everything* I could think of to repel the ghost or demon or whatever it is. And it ignored them like they were just toys."

"Did it hurt you?"

"No, but—"

"Then there you have it," I say. I nod and smile at one of the kids on my football team, trying to seem cool and nonchalant and not at all worried that someone is going to ask about how sleepless I look or overhear this very strange conversation. "You were alone and you made it out okay. Now we're surrounded by people. Nothing to worry about. And April and Andres aren't alone either."

They always feel the strongest when you're alone.

Immediately, I'm no longer in the school hallway.

I stand in the living room, and Dad is drunk. My blood chills as the memory overtakes me. As my mom goes to the garage to get a shop vacuum because Dad has broken a beer bottle all over the carpet. Snakes writhe and twine through the shattered glass. Dad doesn't even seem to notice he's broken something. He thunders around, yelling about work or Mom or me, I can't really tell at this point.

I also can't move.

I feel frozen.

I know if I move, he'll come after me. I know if I move, the snakes will attack. I've seen Dad in this state before, when his face is red and his fists are clenched. He wants to fight. All he needs is for a target to present itself.

Dad roars and curses and slams his fist into the wall. It breaks through the drywall easily. It's not the first spot we've had to cover with a picture frame.

The last was a photo of the three of us, all pretending to be one happy family. The irony has always tasted bitter in my throat.

Even though I expect it, I still yelp and flinch back on the sofa, where I've been sitting for the last few hours. We'd all been watching TV together. Fine and happy. But a dozen beers in, and Dad stopped being either of those, and now I have nowhere to go but here.

Dad turns and looks at me. His red face twists into a scowl.

And that's when I am acutely aware that Mom is outside, out of earshot, and I am in here.

"You," he growls.

He starts cursing. Calling me terrible names I try to drown out but that will stick to my subconscious forever.

He steps toward me. Snakes curl and hiss at his feet.

"No," I whisper, and it's then that I feel myself, still standing in the school hall, watching this memory unfold like a nightmare's black wings. "Please."

Dad's arm cocks back, a snake curled around his bicep, and I wince in fear.

I feel his hand on my arm. Yanking me off the couch.

Only the punch never comes.

The hand on my arm doesn't let go, and after a moment I realize that the voice saying my name over and over isn't my dad's, but Deshaun's.

"Dude," he says, shaking me. "Kyle, what's wrong?"

I open my eyes. Why did I shut my eyes? Why was I flinching from something that happened months ago?

I swallow hard as the bustle and roar of the crowded hallway comes back. I stare around at my classmates with wide eyes.

What just happened?

That wasn't just a memory. That was real.

"I . . ." I whisper. I look to Deshaun, who stares at me with wide, nervous eyes.

I can't finish the statement. I can tell from his look he doesn't need me to. We both know what's going on.

"Come on," he says. "Let's get to class."

He doesn't say we'll be safe there.

He doesn't tell me to face my fears.

He is silent.

And as he leads me toward our next room, I swear I see the clown in the crowd, staring at me with those cold blue eyes and a smile on his face.

The clown knows.

The clown knows.

Deshaun

I watch Kyle all through chemistry. We're lab partners, so we sit together, but even though he's right beside me, he seems like he's a thousand miles away. He keeps staring at the corners of the room, or looking out the window, like he's waiting to see a ghost.

Even though it's really *me* who's waiting for that.

I know I need to talk to him about his dad. For the last few years, I've seen things in his house get worse and worse, but he's never admitted to anything. We've all been too scared to talk about it. Too scared to face the truth. I mean, I don't know for certain that things are bad at home, but I can guess. I used to stay at his all the time, and now he rarely invites me over, and only when his dad isn't there. And the note he got . . . *You can't escape the fear you live with.*

That *has* to mean his dad. And I have to help him.

As our teacher describes saponification, I jot down a list of things that might help keep us safe. Various charms or crystals, weird chants, hiding our mirrors, different types of incense. But every single one of those seems sillier than the last.

I thought I'd find my answers in books, but it turns out that life is nothing like a book. In books, things always come to a neat conclusion. They make sense. Life isn't always like that, and I'm terrified that this is one of those times.

No matter how much I prepare, I'll never be able to fend off the clown. It will continue to chase us all down until we die of fright.

I think of April. The way her eyes lit up when I said I was trying to figure out how to end this thing.

I have to protect her. I have to protect all of them.

"You can't protect them," growls a voice to my right.

I look over, goose bumps racing down my arms. It's Vanessa, one of my classmates, only it isn't her voice that I hear. I stare at her in shock as her head twists to face me; no other limb in her body moves. The motion is unearthly. Her eyes are white.

"*You can't even protect yourself,*" Vanessa-who-is-not-Vanessa says.

Fear and bile rise in the back of my throat. I swallow them both down and look around. Is anyone else seeing this?

No one else in the room is talking. Everything is frozen—our teacher holds a marker to the whiteboard; Kyle's stuck chewing absentmindedly on a pen; even the sky outside seems paused.

And in that moment, I know that there is nothing I can think of to defeat or protect myself from this evil force. It can make the very world stand still—what chance do a bag of salt and some charms have against that?

"What do you want?" I ask. My voice wavers. Honestly, I'm impressed I can even talk.

"*Your fear,*" Vanessa growls. She leans over, her movements jerky. "*I want to drain every last drop of fear from you. All of you. Until you are nothing but husks!*"

"I won't let you."

The words leave my mouth before I can stop them,

before I can even register how stupid it is to be taunting an enemy like this. Everything I thought before was wrong. I'm surrounded by people, and the evil is still here. I'm facing my fear, and it isn't going away. I force myself to think of Kyle, April, and Andres. I can't let them get hurt. I can't let any of us get hurt.

"I'm going to stop you," I say.

"And how will you do that?" she asks with a laugh.

I push myself to standing. The chair screeches against the floor, but not even that makes the world break back into motion. For all the people around us, it is just me and my fear.

"You can't hurt us," I say. "All you can do is try to scare us. Well, I refuse to be scared. Not anymore!"

I don't know what I expect. I hope she'll howl and the ghost will vanish because I've stood up to it.

She opens her mouth. I wait for the scream.

Instead, she starts to laugh. It's the sound of breaking glass and nails on a chalkboard. It takes all my control not to cover my ears.

"Is that so?" she asks when she's finished cackling.

Vanessa-not-Vanessa stands like a puppet being yanked by its strings.

"*You think you can face me? You think I can't touch you?*" She reaches out and touches my cheek. Her nail scratches my skin, and I flinch back. "*You think I can't hurt you?*"

Her smile is more terrifying than anything I've seen so far. It splits her face, almost as wide as the clown's, and her eyes now glow blue.

"*Let me show you what I can do.*"

She holds out her hand, her fingers twisted like an open claw right toward my heart. Then she clenches, and my world goes white with pain.

Everything hurts. Every muscle in my body goes tight, pulls past breaking, and I am screaming, screaming, as my limbs tear themselves apart. And it's not just me screaming either—through the blinding light of my pain, I see the others. Kyle fighting off snakes that aren't there. Andres drowning on solid ground. And April running for her life as the clown gets closer and closer.

It's not just my friends either who I see failing to fight their demons. At the edges, hidden in light, are my siblings, my parents, my other classmates, stretching out into infinity.

*"You are just the beginning. When I have your
fear, I will bring out others' as well!"*

The pain becomes too much.

I collapse to the ground, and the horrifying vision
collapses with it.

The pain, however, stays.

"Deshaun!" Kyle says. He kneels at my side, and
it takes far too long for reality to fade in. I'm back in
the classroom. It's silent once more, but not because
of magic or a ghost. It's silent because I am collapsed
on the ground by my desk, and the entire class is cir-
cled around me, save for the teacher.

"Mr. Lyle went to get the nurse," Vanessa says
reassuringly. I flinch back from her, my mind still
reeling with the image of her blank white eyes.

"I'm okay," I say.

"Don't," Kyle says. He keeps a steady hand on my
shoulder, keeping me on the ground. "Don't move.
Just in case you hurt yourself."

"How . . . What . . ."

"You just started screaming," Kyle says. "And
then you passed out."

His voice is quiet, but I can tell he's scared. He's

trying to play it cool around our classmates. He knows the truth.

I close my eyes.

Distantly, I hear Mr. Lyle come back and tell everyone to step aside. Everyone does, save for Kyle.

"Did you see it?" Kyle whispers.

I nod my head.

"I was wrong. So wrong," I say. The nurse comes over and helps me to sit up, but I don't open my eyes. I don't want to see any of this.

I don't know what I'll see.

"It *can* hurt us," I say. I open my eyes then and stare straight at Kyle. "You have to warn them. They aren't safe. None of us are."

Mr. Lyle and the nurse lift me to my feet and take me away.

Andres

The stubbled concrete is wet and cold against my bare feet.

All around me my classmates giggle and talk nervously, their voices echoing within the pool room. Pretty much everyone has wrapped themselves in their towels, covering as much bare skin as they can. No one has jumped in. Mostly because we all know the pool is kept regulation temp, which means freezing cold.

I don't want to get in at all. Not for the first time, I consider April's advice of pretending to be sick.

I stand here, alone, and stare at the swimming pool. She's in social studies right now, safe and warm and dry, and all I can do is think about what Deshaun said: We're safe so long as we aren't alone. The clown can only scare us. Not hurt us.

Just scare.

Trouble is, I'm pretty certain it's 100 percent possible to be scared to death.

"Come on, guys," the gym teacher, Mr. Lonergan, yells out. "Everyone in the pool!"

He blows a whistle, and, reluctantly, we all throw our towels on the bleachers—the air almost feels as cold as the pool will feel.

The kids around me all jump in, splashing and yelping at how cold it is.

I stand on the edge, frozen, and look into the water.

I know there aren't any sharks in swimming pools. I know that just doesn't happen. It's never happened. It never will happen. And if for some reason it does happen, the odds of it happening in my middle school swimming pool are infinitesimally small.

I know all this.

I know how to think rationally.

But it's like there's another part of my brain now, the part that doesn't care about things like possible and probable. And that part of my brain is screaming, telling me: *Just because you can see the bottom doesn't mean the depths aren't hiding something sinister.*

"Come on, Andres," Mr. Lonergan says. He steps up beside me. "Hop on in. The water won't bite."

I look up at him. Does he know what he just insinuated? He smiles at me. And there's nothing really scary in that smile, but for the briefest moment, I swear his eyes flash pale blue.

"Either that or sit out and get an F for the day," he says. He shrugs. "Choice is yours."

I look between him and the water. Just staring at the pool makes me shiver, and not from the temperature. Who knows what's waiting in there? But if it's a matter of facing a cold pool or facing an angry mother demanding to know why I failed an easy class like gym, I'll take the pool.

It only wants to scare us. It only wants to scare us.

I dip my toe in the water.

It's colder than I thought.

Then, before I can second-guess, I jump in.

Freezing water rushes around me, and I thrash to the surface with a gasp.

When I do, I'm no longer in the swimming pool.

"No," I whisper.

Cold, salty water sneaks into my mouth. I cough.

I am in the middle of the ocean.

Water stretches as far as I can see. Cold, slate-blue water and a cloudy gray sky. My heart immediately starts hammering in my chest. I turn around, treading water frantically. No shore behind me. No land anywhere.

Just an endless blanket of water and a cold, unforgiving sky.

"Help!" I yell.

My voice doesn't echo like it would in the gym. My cry gets swallowed by the emptiness around me. And that's when I know—this isn't a hallucination or vision. I've been transported to the ocean, and if I don't get out quick, I'm going to drown. My limbs are already so cold that swimming is getting difficult. I don't have time to figure out what happened or why. My only thought is how I'm going to escape.

"Somebody, help!" I call out. Nothing. *"Please!"*

My mind conjures up all sorts of terrible things that could be swimming below and around me, just waiting to brush against my legs or nibble on my feet.

Jellyfish or giant squid.

Or sharks.

Of course, sharks.

Fresh goose bumps crawl over my body.

I go to call out for help again, but my mouth fills with salt water. I sputter and choke, kick harder to remain afloat. I'm thrashing so hard, it would be impossible not to see me.

I see it then. On the horizon.

A shape cutting through the water, materializing through the mirage line between sky and sea. A boat. And it's heading straight toward me.

I wave my arms wildly, throwing up waves.

It has to see me. It *has* to.

The ship keeps getting larger, growing closer. Tall and gray and grand, probably the size of an ocean liner. It slices through the waves, tossing up sprays of white.

It's coming fast.

Too fast.

The boat draws nearer.

It's *not* a boat.

It's a shark fin. And it is larger than anything I've ever seen.

"HELP!" I scream out.

I begin to swim. Paddling as hard and as fast as I can. Away from the giant monster closing in behind me. My breath screams in my lungs and my limbs are getting slower, heavier.

When I glance back, I see the shark is nearer now.

The top half of its body is above the water. Larger than a submarine and faster, parting waves the size of houses. Its beady black eyes are locked on me.

It opens its mouth.

A silent roar.

Its jaws are huge. Its bloody teeth larger than skyscrapers.

I know then that I'm not going to escape.

I'm

   never

      going

      to escape.

I try to swim harder.

My body fails me.

My arms are tired. Gelatinous. I flop through the water.

I glance back once more at the shark.

I can smell the stink of its breath. The roar of its hungry jaws.

I am going to die.

I close my eyes.

Let myself sink under the water.

I don't want to see this. Just want it to be over.

And something grabs me by the arm, pulls me back up. Onto cold, wet concrete.

"Andres!" Mr. Lonergan yells out. "Andres, are you okay?"

I blink open my eyes. Cough up water.

I don't taste salt.

I taste chlorine.

I'm in the pool room. I'm safe and in school and everything is okay.

"What happened?"

"You just started thrashing," the teacher says. "I thought you knew how to swim!"

"I . . ."

I look over to the pool. To the still, safe indoor pool. All of my classmates stare at me. No one speaks.

"I think I better go to the nurse," I manage to say.

"Yeah," Mr. Lonergan replies. "Yeah, I think that would be a good idea."

He drapes a towel over me and helps me shakily stand. I pull the towel around tight. I'm cold. So cold.

And scared.

So scared.

That shark was real.

I know it was real.

If it had caught me, I'd be dead.

A shudder rips through my body, almost taking me to my knees, but the teacher's arm around my shoulders helps keep me upright.

"It's okay, big guy," Mr. Lonergan says. He looks down at me and smiles. Sharp teeth. A smile too wide for his face. And his eyes burning blue as fire. "I'm only just starting to have fun with you."

Kyle

I don't leave Deshaun's side.

We sit together in the nurse's office while she takes his temp and looks at his pupils and checks his head for injuries.

"Are you sure you don't remember what happened?" she asks.

Deshaun shakes his head. His dark face has paled, and his eyes are even more bloodshot than they were this morning. I know the look she's giving him—she's wondering if she should send him to the hospital to run tests. And I know that's the last place he should be right now. Alone and isolated and defenseless.

"He told me he didn't get any sleep last night," I interject. "Or the night before."

"Are you not feeling okay?" the nurse asks, concerned.

"Video games," I respond for him.

The nurse raises an eyebrow. "Video games?"

"Yeah," Deshaun says. He looks over to me, then lowers his eyes with fake guilt. "I got a new one on Friday and haven't stopped playing until, well, until this morning."

The nurse tsks. "That would explain it. Prolonged staring at a screen and sleep deprivation isn't a good combination. I'm sure you haven't been eating well either. All that Halloween candy." She touches his forehead again, as if to make sure he doesn't have a fever. "I think the best thing I can do for you right now is to send you home. I'll call your parents."

"They're at work," I say. "I can take him home, though. He's only a few blocks away."

"You're not getting out of class, Kyle," the nurse says.

"No, I know. I'll be back before next period. Please? I want to make sure he gets home safe."

I have no doubt that the nurse wants to say no. I have no doubt that this goes entirely against protocol. I am quickly thinking of excuses or ways I can convince her when the door to the nurse's office slams open suddenly and a kid walks in, his face green as spinach.

"I'm sick," the kid says. The moment the words leave his mouth, he starts to throw up.

The nurse leaps into action, grabbing a bucket and trying to contain the mess.

"Go, just go," she says to us. "Get some rest, Deshaun. I'll tell your teachers you won't be back. Kyle, you have thirty minutes. Go!"

Deshaun and I look at each other and try to contain our surprise. How in the world did we manage to get out of school that easily? It makes me think we should have tried this sooner. When not running from killer clowns. I help him off the cot where he's been sitting, and together we hastily make our way out the door, stepping over the puddles as we go.

"What happened in there?" I ask as soon as we're outside. My excitement over getting out of class quickly vanishes with the weight of *why* I'm out here in the first place: Something terrible happened to Deshaun. And if it happened to him, it could happen to any of us.

Deshaun doesn't answer.

"Deshaun—" I begin.

"You don't want to know," he interrupts. He looks at me, and the fear in his eyes tells me everything. He is correct: I don't want to know what he saw. "Where are we going?" he asks.

"Your house," I say. "You need to sleep."

"No!" he yells. Much more forcefully than I think he intends. He shakes his head. "Sorry. I just . . . I can't go back there. Not after what happened. I don't think it's safe for us to wait around. This thing. Whatever it is, it's getting violent. It's getting more powerful. It can hurt us now. We need to get rid of it."

"But how?"

"I don't know," he admits. "But we need to get to the others before something bad happens to them."

I nod and pull out my phone to text Andres.

I can only hope it's not too late.

Caroline

The classroom closes in. The walls are dirt. The floor is dirt. The windows are dirt. Even the air in my lungs is dirt.

It squeezes around me, and I can't breathe, can't breathe.

But I sit there, quietly, as the grave crushes against my chest.

There is no point crying. No one will come.

No one will ever come back.

April

Andres is waiting for me outside the door when my class is finished. His eyes are nervously darting around to the kids who walk past us, and his hair drips down his face unchecked.

"You aren't checking your phone," he says the moment he sees me. He almost sounds angry, but he's definitely more scared. He takes my arm and pulls me down the hall. Not toward lunch, but toward the exit.

"I was in class," I say defensively. "Why? Where are we going?"

He doesn't say anything. His face is set in grim determination.

"I'm not staying here," he grumbles. He reaches

into his pocket and pulls out his phone. "I was nearly eaten in gym class. And it sounds like I'm not the only one."

He hands his phone over to me.

It's a conversation with Kyle. And as I read it, my stomach drops.

"Deshaun was sent to the nurse's office," I whisper. I hand him back the phone. "He tried facing the ghost and it attacked him. And wait, what do you mean you were nearly eaten?"

He glances at me.

"Glad I'm at the top of your priorities." His voice is rough. "In gym. We were swimming. And suddenly it wasn't the pool, but the ocean, and the biggest shark you've ever seen was coming after me. I nearly died. Until Mr. Lonergan pulled me out, but I think he was actually the clown in disguise, or possessed, or I don't know. I don't know what's going on anymore, only that we can't trust anyone and this thing is getting worse. It can control our reality—our fears let it in, and it can shift everything. Which is bad enough—but now it's getting violent."

"So what are we going to do?"

"Not be split up anymore, for one thing," he says.

I fully expect a teacher to yell at us when we cross the threshold to the school and step out into the cold afternoon air. After all, we're breaking a ton of rules. But maybe it's the general chaos of kids rushing between classes—no one calls out. No one stops us. It almost feels easy. Too easy.

Until . . .

"Hey!" Andres calls. He nods toward the flagpole. To the girl sitting there with her head in her hands. I know who it is before she even looks at us.

Caroline.

She looks terrible, and while that might have made me feel good a few days ago, now I actually feel bad. Her makeup streaks down her face and her eyes are puffy and red. I can tell even from here that her breath is fast and frantic, like a rabbit running from a fox.

And it's then I know, before she even opens her mouth, that she was lying to us before.

She *has* been facing some sort of evil. And it hasn't been kind to her.

As much as I don't like it, we're in this together.

Caroline doesn't call back or even move, really. She just stares at us without really seeing. We pause in front of her, Andres still holding my arm.

"Are you okay?" he asks.

She swallows. She doesn't answer.

Andres looks at me. Nods at her. I know that expression: *She used to be your friend. Say something!*

"Caroline, um." I look around and kneel down, putting my hands on her knees. She looks at me, her eyes glazed over, and sniffs. "Caroline, if this is about what happened in the graveyard . . . or whatever happened *after* the graveyard, you're not alone. We're being haunted too. It's been coming after all of us. But we think that together, we can face it." I squeeze her knee. "We can defeat it."

She shakes her head. "No." Her voice is so quiet I barely hear it. "You can't defeat this. It's inevitable. It comes for all of us." She starts to cry. "Sometimes it comes too soon."

I look up at Andres. He shrugs.

"Caroline," Andres says, "we're going to go meet Deshaun and Kyle, who were also there that night. We're all going to tackle this thing, because it's not going to stop until we defeat it. And I think . . . I think you need to come with us."

"What?" I ask.

Andres doesn't back down. "Caroline is a part of this." He doesn't say more, but I know the rest: *whether we like it or not.*

"You're right," I say. "Together, we can do it."

It doesn't matter that none of us has any idea what we're actually doing, but being together feels like a sort of plan. It feels better than just sitting around and waiting for the clown to strike again.

I stand and hold out my hand to Caroline.

"Come on," I say. "Let's go. It's time we ended this, once and for all."

She looks up at me. Then Andres. And for the first time this entire exchange, she looks like she actually sees us.

"Okay," she says finally. "Together."

She takes my hand. Her palm is wet with her tears.

When I pull her up to standing, I see a kid by the swing set.

He stares at us.

And when he sees me looking back, his eyes flash blue.

And his smile
    stretches

                ear
                        to
                                ear.
He waves.
I turn and start to run.

Deshaun

"What are we going to do?" Kyle asks for the millionth time.

We stand at the main entrance to the graveyard, the big gate stretching up behind us, pitch-black iron against a pale blue sky. April and Andres should be here soon. The world seems far too bright for all of this. Shouldn't it be dark and stormy? Shouldn't the terrible monsters only come out after midnight?

Kyle looks around, and I know he isn't just running from snakes or a clown.

Not all monsters wait until midnight.

"Are you okay?" I ask.

Kyle swallows. "I'm being chased by a killer clown who puts snakes in my bed. What do you think?"

"That's not what I mean," I reply. I don't say anything more. I don't know what else *to* say.

Kyle looks at me. Things seem to click behind his eyes, and he looks away again.

"I want to say this is the most scared I've ever been," I say. I glance back to the graveyard. "But honestly . . . that night I got stuck in the graveyard, that was the worst."

I've never really talked about that night. Not even to Kyle, who was my best friend back then, just like now. He'd been sick the night of the hide-and-seek.

"I've never felt so alone," I say quietly. "I couldn't find my way out, and no matter how much I called out, no one came. Until I started hearing . . ." I gulp and look back to the graves. "Until I started hearing the ghosts. They followed me everywhere. And they kept saying such terrible things. Like I would never escape, and no one cared, and I would be lost there forever."

Kyle is biting his lip, staring down at his shoes.

"I had no idea," he says.

"Because I was too scared to tell you. I thought if

I did, you'd make fun of me. It was bad enough that everyone else was laughing. I couldn't stand the idea that you would too."

"I would never."

"I know. And you never did. And that helped. You just being there, never bringing it up. You helped me forget about it. But now . . . now I can't forget about it anymore. I have to face it. I was too scared to, before. But with you and Andres and April, I don't feel so afraid. I don't feel like I'm facing it on my own."

I reach over and squeeze his shoulder.

"We're all facing scary things," I continue. "When we went to high school, I started to feel like I was alone in the graveyard again. I thought you were getting distant. You know, not inviting me over as much, doing all the sports. I thought it was because you were getting too cool to hang out with me."

He finally looks back to me, and I know then he realizes I'm not just talking about the snake or the clown or high school. I'd always been too scared to ask if things were okay at home, because I didn't know how I could help. But now, we both have to fight our fears. Our *true* fears.

"That's not why I was distant. He's getting

meaner," Kyle says. His eyes fill with tears, but he blinks them down. "I was doing everything I could to stay out of the house. I don't know how much more I can take. Before it gets really bad." He looks down.

I swallow. It's the very last thing I want to hear. Now that it's said, there's no hiding from it.

"I didn't know it was that bad," I whisper. "I'm so sorry. You're not alone. What can I do to help?"

Kyle shakes his head.

"I don't know," he whispers. I've known him most of my life. And I've never, ever heard him sound this scared.

I pull him in for a hug.

"It's okay," I say, more gently. I feel awkward and don't know what's the right thing to do or say. Because it's not okay. None of this is even remotely okay. But I want him to know I'm here for him through it.

He continues to not say anything. I step back, but I don't let go of his shoulder.

"When this is over," I say. I pause. Will this be over? What could I possibly do or say to make this better? "When this is over, you can come stay at mine. You'll never have to see him again. I swear it. My parents love you. They'll totally adopt you."

"I don't think it works like that," he says. His voice sounds full of gravel.

"I don't care," I reply. "I'll make it work like that."

He finally looks at me. Finally. For real. And he's no longer the friend I thought I was losing because he was getting too cool. He's Kyle. My best friend, Kyle.

"We have to get through this first," he says.

I nod. If nothing else, I feel resolute. I *will* figure this out. To save him. To save April. To save all of us.

"We will," I say.

He wipes away his tears and nods to the road.

"They're here."

I glance over. And sure enough, there are Andres and April—and beside them is someone I never thought I'd see with them in a million years. Caroline.

"What's she doing here?" Kyle asks when they arrive. His voice is still gruff, but now it just makes him sound angry.

"She's a part of this," April says defensively. "She's being haunted too."

Kyle holds up his hands in surrender.

"All good," he says. "Sorry. I think we're all just on edge."

April nods. Kyle looks to Andres. Reaches out and brushes his wet hair with a finger.

"What happened to you?" he asks, much more gently.

"Shark in the swimming pool," Andres replies. He says it so matter-of-factly that I almost chuckle. Almost. Except he's definitely, deadly serious about it.

Kyle nods.

April looks to me.

"What do we do now?" she asks.

It's the question I've been fearing. Because I don't have an answer. I only have what the stories have told me to do, and so far, the stories have all lied. Facing our fears didn't do anything but get me hurt, and I have a terrible feeling that it will only get worse.

"I'm not really sure," I admit. I want to apologize for letting them down, for not knowing what to do. Then I look at Kyle and remember our talk. Maybe this isn't just about facing our fears or understanding them. "I thought at first . . . I thought maybe we just needed to face our fears. But maybe it's more than that. Maybe we have to stand up to them. Prove that we're no longer afraid."

"There's no way I can stand up to a shark," Andres says. He drops down to a crouch. "We're doomed. We are so totally doomed."

"I mean, at least you just have to worry about sharks," April says. "All you have to do is stay out of the water."

"All water!" Andres yelps. "With my luck, I'm going to have a shark jump out of my drinking glass tonight."

I can't help it; I giggle a little bit. Andres looks at me, and for a moment I think he's going to be angry, but then he grins sheepishly.

"I guess this means I have a good reason not to shower anymore, though. Right?"

"You do," Kyle says, clearly on his side. "Though maybe a shower now and then . . ."

We all laugh, but there isn't a lot of humor in it. If we don't do something soon, none of us will be alive long enough to worry about things like showering.

"We have to defeat this. We have to face our fears and put them to rest," I say. "Together. The five of us. Somehow."

"Maybe we can go back to the grave?" April asks. "Maybe there's another clue. Something we missed."

"There's nothing there," Kyle says. "We've looked it over a dozen times."

An idea sparks in my head. I turn to Caroline. She looks like she's only hearing half the conversation— she has her arms crossed tight around her chest, gripping her shoulders like she's freezing cold.

"Caroline," I say. "Did you take something that first night? From the box. In the grave."

"I . . ." she begins. She looks everywhere but at me. Then she unclenches her hands from her shoulders and reaches into her pocket, pulling out a small folded piece of paper.

She hands it over to me without a word.

I glance around at the others, who have all huddled in. They nod for me to open it.

I do.

It's a photograph.

A woman. She's familiar . . .

"Who is this?" I ask.

I look up to Caroline. She stares up at the graveyard with fear and pain clear on her face.

"My mom," she whispers after a while. "That was . . . that was supposed to be the photo from her obituary."

April

Caroline's statement is a punch to the chest. I look around, but my friends seem just as shocked as I do.

"When did . . .?" I ask. I can't finish the question. I had no idea her mother passed away.

"Last year," she replies. "Just after summer break started."

"I didn't know," I whisper.

"No one did," she replies. "My dad decided not to run the obituary at the last minute. Didn't want anyone to know. He didn't want anyone to pity us."

I can only stare at her in shock.

Is this why she acted so mean to me? She was

hurting. She was hurting because no one knew her pain, and she had no way of reaching out.

"I'm sorry," I say.

Two words I never thought I'd say to her, once we broke apart. Now I mean them more than ever.

I go on. "I had no idea. I wish I did. I would have been there for you."

My friends echo the sentiment.

The spell on her seems to break, just a little—when she looks at me, her eyes are clear.

"Thank you," she says. "That . . . that means a lot. Really."

She takes a deep breath and steadies herself.

"I think I know what we need to do," she says. "At least, where we need to start."

"Really?" I ask.

She nods. "Deshaun said that we need to stand up to our fears, right? Well, ever since my mom died and I saw her buried, I've been terrified to go back to her grave. That's what this . . . this *thing* . . . has been showing me over and over. The grave. The feeling of dirt closing in. I haven't been able to sleep since we visited here. I keep thinking I'm being buried alive." She pauses, looks to the graveyard. "This is the graveyard where she was buried. Maybe we need to start here."

"Are you sure?" I ask. I put a hand on her shoulder. She doesn't shrug it off. "I mean, that's a lot. I totally understand if you don't want to do this."

She nods, resolute. "I'm sure. I need to put this to rest. All of it."

Caroline

This is the last place I want to be.

This is the last place I want to be, yet here I am, with the last people I thought I'd be with, trudging up the long, winding drive toward the place that has haunted me every moment of my life for the last year.

Every step, and I feel the walls of dirt closing in.

Every breath, and I feel the gravel clogging my lungs.

But I refuse to stop. I refuse to give in.

I want to remember my mom the right away. Her laughter and her smiles and the amount of love she had for me. I don't want to remember her like this, don't want to relate her to so much fear and pain.

I am going to end this fear.

I look to April.

We are going to end this.

I never thought of asking her or any of them for help. I knew they had been facing *something* after that night in the graveyard. But this last year, I had learned to be alone. Until I realized there was no way to face this on my own.

I've been trying all this time.

I've been failing.

I take them to the one place in this entire graveyard I'm afraid to go. The one place I worried the note I received would lead me. Not back to the grave with the jack-o'-lantern and the secrets. Someplace far more terrifying. At least for me.

My mother's grave sits in a small grove of trees.

She loved the forest. My dad wanted her to always feel like she was in one.

We reach her grave and I can barely stand. I slouch heavily against April. She doesn't say anything. She doesn't complain. She doesn't let go.

I stare at the headstone.

HERE LIES THE BODY

My vision swims.

I can't be reading that correctly.

I blink, rub my hands over my eyes.

No. No way.

HERE LIES THE BODY OF CAROLINE KNOWLES

"It's time," comes a voice. My heart drops when I hear it.

"Mom?"

She stands at my side, wearing a long white dress. Her hair hangs heavy around her shoulders, as if she was caught in the rain. She looks exactly as I remember.

When she looks at me, though, her eyes flash blue.

It must just be the light.

"Yes, sweetie. It's time for you to join me. I miss you, sweetie. I want you to come home."

My heart aches so badly I drop to my knees.

"What do you mean?" I ask. But I know what she means.

The visions of the grave closing in.

The memory of the day I lost her, when that first clump of dirt echoed on top of her casket, when the earth swallowed her down. It had been cool and blue outside. Just like this. I had been surrounded by people but so, so alone. Just like this.

"It's time, Sunnybunny. My angel. You've fought so hard. But now you can rest. You can rest with me."

I don't know where she pulls it from, but she hands me a shovel. It glints in the sun like a smile. Like her smile.

"You know what to do, sweetie. Join me. Join me."

He smile widens. I feel the weight of the shovel in my hands and watch her eyes burn blue.

She steps behind me, puts her hands on my shoulders.

She leans over and whispers in my ear.

"You are worth nothing without me. I was the only one who loved you. Everyone else is just pretending."

I see her reflected in the shovel's blade.

But it isn't my mother I see.

It is the clown.

His mouth red and split in a smile that slashes his face. His eyes burning blue like the hottest part of fire.

"Do it," he says. And now I hear it is his voice.

The same clown I saw when leaving the grave-yard. The same one I've seen in passing reflections, in faces in the crowd. The one I know has been haunting not just me, but all of us. Toying with us.

I'm not going to be haunted or toyed with anymore.

"No!" I yell.

I go to stand, to spin around and knock the clown down.

When I move, the clown is no longer there.

The vision or hallucination shatters.

I stand on my mother's grave, a stick in my hands, and look at the kids who joined me. My friends. The clown or the ghost of my mother is nowhere to be seen.

April jerks forward, as if suddenly unfrozen. The rest follow shortly after, shaking themselves and staring around wildly.

"What was that?" April asks. "What did you do? The clown . . . I saw you talking to the clown, but we couldn't move."

"It tried to convince me to dig my own grave." I can barely finish the sentence. "It wanted me to think it was my mom. It wanted me to give up on everything." I swallow hard and force myself to smile. "I think it's scared. I think we're close."

Deshaun isn't really paying attention to us. He's staring behind me, his eyes wide.

"I think you're right," he says, his voice terrified. "But I don't think we're close—I think we're here."

I turn around.

My mother's grave is gone.

Instead, the thick trees around us tower and arch in. Stones of old grave markers poke up from their roots. And there, amid the tangled mass of root and dirt and old graves, is a cave bored straight into the earth.

Deeper in, a pale blue light beckons.

I stare into it. I can already feel the earth closing in around me. No part of me wants to go in there.

I clench the stick that the clown tricked me with.

Deep in my heart, I know:

My mother would not want me to give up.

She would not want me to lose her forever by burying all my memories beneath fear and loss.

She would not want me to think I'm alone.

No.

She would want me to fight.

"Okay," I say. I tighten my fists. "Let's go."

PART FOUR
the grave

Deshaun

"Are we really going in there?" Kyle asks.

I keep looking around, expecting the clown to pop out at any second to scare us. But the birds chirp in the sky and the cave beckons darkly. I know we don't have a choice. This is where it all ends.

And I don't have any clue how it's going to end for us.

I still have no clue how to defeat the monster.

April steps up to my side. She takes my hand. Her fingers shake, and for a moment the movement shocks me. Then I realize she isn't holding my hand to comfort me, but to be comforted. I squeeze. Her hand is warm, and when she looks at me, she smiles faintly.

It's then that I realize it doesn't matter if we don't know how to face down this ghost or monster or whatever it is. We are together. Finally. And we are going to end this. One way or another.

"Yeah," I say. "We're going in."

I pull out my phone, turn on the flashlight, and lead the way down into the dark.

"What do you think is down here?" April whispers.

"I don't know," I respond. "But we're going to find out."

She nods, as if that's answer enough.

Caroline, Kyle, and Andres are behind us. I glance back once. They all have phones out, casting harsh white light over the walls.

Even though we've only moved a few feet, the exit is already gone, replaced by a wall of dirt. My breath catches.

We're trapped.

I keep my mouth shut, though. Try to look brave.

"We can do this," I say.

They all nod at me, but they don't seem to buy it. Kyle raises an eyebrow at me holding April's hand, and I feel myself blush in spite of our surroundings.

"Whatever we do," I say, looking forward once

more, "we have to stick together. Remember, this thing feeds on our fear, and we're more vulnerable when alone. So no matter what, we don't. Split. Up."

No response. They must just be scared to talk; I don't blame them—this place seems to drain all life and happiness from me. It makes me want to curl against the wall and hide.

It's so quiet, all noise feels like throwing a great shiny target up in the air that says "Attack me!"

Wait.

It's so quiet.

I can't hear their footsteps anymore. Did they stop? The moment the question crosses my mind, April lets go of my hand.

"Guys?"

I pause. Reach back for April's hand. She takes it.

"Why are we stopping?" I ask as I look back.

"They're lost," comes a voice. "Alone." I glance over. Fear courses through my veins.

The clown stands beside me, gripping my hand tight.

"Just like you," he growls.

Andres

One moment I'm surrounded by friends.

The next footstep, and the cave goes dark—my phone blinks off and the light at the end vanishes.

The next thing I realize is: I'm alone.

Completely alone.

"Guys?" I yell out. My voice echoes. As if I'm in a large cave. I reach my hands out to the sides in the pitch-blackness—I can't see my own fingers, let alone the walls, and I can't feel anything either. I take a tentative step forward. My foot squishes in mud.

I freeze.

Hold my breath.

The ground was dry before.

Immediately my heart starts to race, because in the distance I hear the
> drip
>> drip
>>> drip
>>>> of water.

All you have to do is stay out of the water, April had said. And when I hear the slosh of waves, I know that that is the last thing I will be able to do.

Deshaun said we need to stand up to our fears.

I'd hoped he was wrong about that.

I don't hear anything else for a while. Just the drip of water and the churn of waves.

Then, slowly but surely, I see a light.

Dim, hazy, the air above me begins to glow. Like millions of tiny stars burning into existence, the ceiling reveals itself. For a moment, all I can think of is how beautiful it is, and how this surely can't be part of the nightmare. Millions and millions of crystals glitter on the cavern ceiling, casting a pale bluish light over everything.

It's that "everything" that makes my stomach churn with newfound fear.

Water.

I am surrounded on all sides by water.

Glittering waves and murky depths. And it's not just the droplets dripping from the ceiling making sound in the waves.

The water isn't empty.

Fins slice through the waves. All sizes, all gray and triangular—some as large as boat sails and others the size of my fist. There must be dozens. *Hundreds.* They swarm and thrash in the waves surrounding my tiny, muddy island.

I turn in place, nearly paralyzed with fear.

Can sharks jump?

There's nowhere to go.

I am stuck on this tiny island.

Forever.

And then

      the ground

      below my feet

         rumbles.

              I gasp

              as inch

                  by

                    inch

      the island

begins

     to

          sink.

Water sloshes up to my toes, soaks through my shoes.

I am alone, and the island is sinking, and the

               sharks

               circle

               in.

Help! I want to cry out. Only I can't speak. I don't want the sharks to hear. I don't want them to know. Besides, there's no one here to help me.

Only . . .

On the far shore, I see another cavern. Blurry, as if behind a pane of frosted glass. And inside . . .

Kyle?

Kyle

Hissing fills my ears.

Snakes slither on every surface.

I can't *see* a surface. Only snakes.

Fat and thin, gray and yellow, green or banded red and black. They writhe around my feet. Twine up my ankles. Drip down from walls.

Walls.

I'm not in the tunnel.

I'm in my house. In the basement.

And there, at the far end, sitting in a high-backed chair, is my father. Around him, the terrariums are open, seething with snakes.

Snakes cover him. They curl up his legs and drape

over his arms, circle their tails over his fingers like rings. A yellow coral snake circles the top of his head in a sinuous crown.

He is the king of my domain.

His eyes burn blue, flash pure hatred at me. He will have my head.

He opens his mouth to speak my name.

A crimson snake, thick as his tongue, slithers out instead.

"*Kyle,*" it whispers in my father's voice, dropping slowly down to my father's lap.

The serpent on my father's crown stares at me, eyes glinting in the ghostly light.

"*Worthlessss,*" the crown hisses.

"*Weak,*" whispers another snake.

"No," I say. I take a step backward and am met with the furious hiss of serpents. I freeze in place. "I'm not," I say. There's no strength behind it.

I'm scared. So scared.

Not only of the snakes.

But because they are right.

Every snake sounds like my father, and as they slither around me, they hiss all the horrible things he's said. All the terrible truths he's told me.

"Freak."

                              "Unlovable."
              "Mistake."

I want to cover my ears, but the serpents curl up
my legs, twine heavy as tree trunks around my arms.

"No son of mine," hisses a cobra by my ear, my
father's voice resonant on its forked tongue.

Serpents everywhere. Cold and biting. Serpents in
my heart, telling me everything I already know.

              "Even your friends despise you."

On his throne, my father watches the snakes surround
me. Watches with that slashed-on grin and burning blue
eyes. I don't think he's ever been happier to see me.

"Where's Deshaun to save you now?" asks a viper
at my waist.

I close my eyes. Try to ignore the cold, scaled bodies that wrap around me. Squeezing me.

I think of Deshaun. My only friend. Always there
to rely on. Always there to help. Always knowing the
answer.

And he is nowhere to be found.

Deshaun

The clown vanishes in a swirl of smoke the moment I see him, leaving me in complete and utter darkness. It's then that I realize my phone is no longer there.

Just me.

Just the dark.

The emptiness.

Only I know, in the deepest pit of my stomach, that I am not alone. I know that I am no longer in the cave.

I feel it first. The race of goose bumps over my skin, the tingle on the back of my neck.

The telltale marks that I am being watched.

"What are you?" I call out to the dark.

Giggling responds, childish and yet somehow ancient, like a soul long trapped in a crypt.

Immediately, my imagination goes haywire.

In the darkness, I see in my mind's eye a little girl, a ghost as pale as a sheet. She floats in front of me with vacant eyes, calling my name. Is it my imagination? Or is she there, floating in the black, just out of arm's reach? Fear floods my veins, cold and spiky.

I take a step back and trip over stone.

Light flickers around me.

I stand in the middle of a graveyard. *The* graveyard. Just like before. Lost and alone but not alone.

Just like before.

The graveyard stretches on into infinity, nothing but burnt grass and gnarled trees and broken tombstones.

And the light . . . the light isn't from the sky, not from any lantern.

The light is from the ghosts.

Hundreds of them, hovering over their tombstones, transparent and pale blue, shining faintly. All of them looking at me with milky eyes.

I take another step backward and am met with a growl.

I turn, shaking, and see a man with his head twisted backward.

"What do you want?" I ask, my voice trembling as I try to find a spot as far away from all of them as I can.

"For you to run," says the little girl. She smiles. Her grin splits her face in two. "Run away, before we scare you to death."

The moment the words leave her mouth, the ghosts all vanish.

And then, like a wolf howling in the night, I hear them wailing. Laughing. Reaching out to me with dirt-crusted nails. Wanting to tear me apart.

I don't think.

I run.

April

"Hello?" I call out.

I can still feel the after trace of Deshaun's hand in mine, but I can't see him anywhere. I can't hear anyone. Can't even tell if I'm still in the tunnel.

Fear grips my heart.

I am alone.

"Hello, April," comes a voice.

I'm not as alone as I thought.

I blink, and the clown stands before me.

We're no longer in the dark of the tunnel, but in my backyard. The sky is cloudy and dark, and there is a table covered in presents and a cake, and we are not alone. My classmates circle us, the clown standing just within the ring. My classmates stare with hatred plain on their faces—squinted eyes and snarled mouths and clenched fists—while the clown . . . the clown just smiles his terrifying smile, his teeth sharp needles and his eyes the only brightness in the otherwise bleak landscape.

"Are you looking for your friends?" the clown asks.

"I . . . I . . ."

The clown's smile somehow grows wider, wider than any human mouth should go. I should be used to this, but I'm not.

"You don't *have* any friends, April." He giggles. "No one wants to be your friend. No one."

"That's a lie," I say. I clench my fists. This is all just a test. This is all just the clown messing with me. And yet, his words sting with the tiny sliver of truth. The question. What if he *isn't* lying?

"Why don't I just let them tell you themselves," the clown says. He bows theatrically. And then, with a jingle of the bells on his shoes, he vanishes.

My classmates remain.

There, right in front of me, is Andres.

Only it doesn't look like Andres, not really—his skin is dull gray and so are his eyes, and when he opens his mouth, his voice sounds like it's coming from the bottom of a well.

"I feel sorry for you, April," Andres says.

"What?"

"That's why I've always stuck around you." He takes a step closer. "I don't actually *like* you. I can't stand being around you! But I feel bad for you, because no one else likes you. It's sad. So sad. And so I'm stuck pretending to be your friend."

"That's not true," I say. I feel tears well at the backs of my eyes. I wipe them away, and when I can see again, the clown is behind Andres, hands on Andres's shoulders, leaning down to whisper in his ear.

"Tell her what you really think," the clown says.

"I think you're boring," Andres says, as if he doesn't even notice the evil clown behind him. "I think you're stupid. So stupid you didn't even realize I was just pretending."

He laughs. It's harsh and cruel, and for some reason, it reminds me of the clown.

The other kids laugh as well.

"You're fat too," calls one of the kids. I look over. It's Caroline, flanked once more by her two stupid friends. "Fat and stupid. You'll never have friends. Let alone a *boyfriend*."

"Yeah," says Deshaun. He steps over to Andres. "You really think I'd like you. Like *that*? No one likes you, April. No one."

I close my eyes and crumple to my knees as my classmates close in.

As they call me terrible names.

As they say all the horrible things I know they've wanted to tell me this entire time.

Caroline

I'm trapped.

I thud my hands against the cushioned roof. No, not a roof—a lid.

I can see from the faint light that seems to come from everywhere and nowhere that I'm in a box. A coffin.

I'm stuck in a coffin.

I struggle and squirm but I can barely move. The coffin is so tight around me.

"*Help*," I gasp. It's barely a whisper. I can't breathe. I can't breathe.

My lungs choke for fleeing oxygen. I'm going to

suffocate. I'm going to suffocate down here and no one will know where I am.

No one will *care*.

I've been horrible. So horrible. Why would anyone care about me? Why would anyone try to save a girl who's bullied them?

Something moves above me.

April?

I slam my hands on the coffin lid once more.

"Help!" I yell, my voice scratchy.

The jingle of bells.

The taunting giggle.

The thud of gravel falling atop the coffin lid.

Another.

And another.

As the clown buries me alive.

Andres

I can see him. Kyle.

In a cave just beyond the lake.

Between the two of us, the lake swarms and froths with sharks. Every second, the island I'm on sinks just a little deeper. Water laps up to my ankles. Smaller sharks—the size of a goldfish—swim past my toes. They haven't bitten me. Yet.

The sharks are hungrier now—some snap at the surface with jaws the size of cars. Others thrash and roil under the water, sending up great waves and the growling crunch of their teeth.

Kyle looks hurt. He crouches on the floor with his hands clasped to his ears. I can't hear him, but I can see his mouth open, screaming at nothing. No, screaming at *something*. Something I can't see, just beyond the cave's entrance.

Somewhere, I know, April is also facing her fear. So is Deshaun. So is Caroline.

"Just stay out of the water," I whisper to myself sarcastically.

I stare at the lake. It seems to spread farther with every passing moment. I remember the pool. The way it stretched to infinity. The way the horizon pulled me back into the waiting jaws of the shark.

Deshaun said we needed to face our fears. Stand up to them.

He said they couldn't really hurt us—even if he'd been hurt by his.

But he's right.

I live in Iowa.

I have no *reason* to be scared of sharks. I've never seen one in real life. I never *will* see one either. This is all in my head. My overactive imagination, my mom would say.

This.

Isn't.

Real.

I swallow down the fear that clogs my throat. Try to steady the furious beat of my heart.

I have to save my friends. I have to help them.

I have to face my fears.

Slowly, cautiously, I step one foot deeper into the water.

The sharks still roil in the waves, circling my sinking island.

I close my eyes.

"This is so stupid," I tell myself in a squeak. I don't know if I mean walking into a shark-infested lake, or fearing sharks at all.

With my eyes still closed, with all my focus on getting to Kyle on the other side, I take another step. This time, my foot doesn't meet ground. I slip off the edge of the island; freezing water sloshes up over my shoulders.

I bite hard on my lips, force my chattering mouth to stay shut as I tread water.

It's all in your head. It's all in your head. There aren't any sharks in Iowa. There aren't any—

Something cold and smooth the size of a bathtub rubs against my thigh.

I can't help it. I yelp.

"It's not a shark," I whisper through chattering teeth. "It's not a real shark."

Another not-shark brushes my other side. Or maybe it's the same one, sizing me up, wondering if I will make a good dinner.

I push the thought aside.

I focus instead on the mental image of my friends. Needing my help. Needing me to face this, so I can help them face their fears.

Keeping my eyes closed, I swim.

With every stroke I expect to feel the crush of teeth on a limb—a shark ripping off an arm, nabbing my foot and pulling me underwater. They slide against me instead, reminding me they are there. I can hear them chomping at air in the distance, can feel the waves from their fins slicing the water just out of reach.

But I don't stop, and the sharks don't bite, and after a while I am so focused on getting to my friends that I barely notice the sharks at all.

My friends are more important.

You can do this, Andres. You can do this.

I swim, and the sharks circle me, and I force myself to stop worrying. I am facing my fear. I am not letting them stop me.

My foot touches land.

I start walking. Sloshing through the waves, brushing aside smaller sharks, my eyes squeezed tight because I still don't want to see them, still don't want to believe what I've done.

When I am fully out of the water, I open my eyes and let out a cry of relief.

I did it!

I faced the sharks.

The tunnel leading to Kyle is right in front of me.

And when I turn around to face the lake, to shout out that I conquered my fears, I am met with a tunnel that stretches back up into darkness.

The lake is no longer there.

I brush my clothes.

My dry clothes.

Maybe the lake was never there in the first place.

Kyle

"Worthless."

"Unwanted."

"You deserve to be punished."

"Nobody will love you."

"Forever alone."

"Forever alone."

"Give in."

"Give in."

"Give in."

"Kyle!"

No, no. Please. Not him too.

"Kyle!" Andres's voice comes again.

I shake my head.

"No," I say.

The serpents twine tighter around me. Dragging me down. Filling my veins with their poison.

My father's words echo in my ears, drowning out everything, a constant hiss plaguing my thoughts. He is right. I am worthless. I deserve to be hurt. I shouldn't fight it anymore.

"You have to fight!" someone calls out. Andres. It sounds like Andres. But no, Andres isn't here. Can't be.

He doesn't like me.

No one likes me.

"Please, Kyle! Fight it off. This isn't real! None of it is real. It's all in your head!"

But he doesn't know the truth. This *is* real. None of this is in my head.

I'm only just now accepting that this is the reality I deserve.

"Fight it, Kyle! For me. For your friends! Think of Deshaun, Kyle. He needs you right now. He needs you to be strong."

"No, no," I say, but I don't know who I'm saying it *to*.

Over the hissing of serpents and crash of my

father's words, I hear footsteps coming close. A hand on my shoulder.

"Fight, Kyle. Come on. Open your eyes. It's me."

I don't want to open my eyes. Because this can't be Andres. This is just another trick. Another trick by my father. To make me hurt. To prove he will always win.

"Come on, Kyle. Please."

It's that word that does it.

My dad never says please. Never.

I open my eyes, expecting the worst.

And Andres is there. Kneeling before me.

Snakes still slither on the floor around us. But they don't cover me. They don't cover him.

"Andres?" I say.

He smiles. "Yes. I just swam across a lake of sharks to get to you. You have to fight this."

"I can't," I say. I can see my father still sitting behind Andres. How does Andres not see him? How does he not see the snakes? "He's too strong. My dad . . . he's right, Andres. He's right. I'm broken. I'm worthless."

I close my eyes again. Andres doesn't let go.

"You're not. I promise you, you're not. You have to face him. You have to believe in yourself. Like I do. Did you hear me before? *I swam through sharks for you.*"

I squeeze my eyes shut.

He believes in me.

He believes in me.

"*He lies,*" hisses my father. "*You are nothing. You will always be nothing. No one cares about you.*"

"You're wrong," I say. My voice is gravelly, rough, but I steel my words. "I'm not nothing. I *do* have friends. Friends who care. Friends who are *nothing* like you!"

I open my eyes. The snakes slither away from me. Retreating. Swarming back toward my father.

I stand on shaky legs. Andres helps me up. I stare down my father and say the words I've wanted to say for so long.

"You're a monster. *You* are the one who's broken. *You* are the one who's unloved. I will never be like you. Do you hear me? I am worthwhile. I am strong. And *I am not afraid of you!*"

I yell the last words, so loud my voice catches.

Serpents twist and twine over my dad's body, as if

they're trying to escape back into him, as if they are scared of *me*.

"I'm not going to let you hurt me anymore," I say. "Never. Again!"

My dad's eyes flash. Bright blue. And when I blink, just for a second, he looks like the clown.

Then he is gone.

I stand there, panting for a long time, leaning heavily against Andres.

"Thank you," I finally say.

He just squeezes my arm.

"Don't mention it. You okay?"

I nod. For once, I actually mean it.

"Good," he says. "Because we still have to find the others. I only hope it's not too late."

April

Everyone is laughing. Laughing and calling me names. *Fat. Stupid. Lazy. Slow.*

Their words blend together, drown out everything, become an oceanic wave that pulls me under, steals my breath. I can't breathe. I hear them all—the people who I thought were my friends, the people who I thought would like me. Andres and Kyle. Caroline. Deshaun.

Deshaun.

Distantly, I remember what Deshaun said, way before we stepped foot in this cursed place.

We'll have to face our fears.

I can see him, behind my eyes.

Face my fears.

I thought I was afraid of the clown. And I am.

But now I realize I was most afraid of this—of being made fun of, of having everyone I know turn against me.

This is worse than the clown.

This must be my biggest fear.

The moment I think that, I feel better. Because if this is the worst situation, if this is what I'm truly afraid of, well . . . I'm surviving.

I open my eyes. Deshaun stares back with his blank expression, his pallid skin. It's not Deshaun at all.

"You're not real," I say. "None of you are."

I push myself to standing and look around at my classmates. No, not my classmates—what I fear of my classmates. The fear that they won't like me. They'll make fun of me. They'll try to hurt me. Just like they did, all those years ago.

Well, I'm done being hurt.

I have real friends. Real friends who care about me. Who are out there fighting their own fears. And I'm not going to let them down by giving in to mine.

"You can't hurt me," I say to Deshaun. "You can't hurt me, because you aren't real."

Instantly, he vanishes, disintegrating like ash in the wind.

They all vanish.

And there, in front of me, standing amid the dust, is the clown.

He is no longer smiling.

His face is twisted into a snarling frown.

"Did you really think it would be that easy?" he growls. "Did you really think you could defeat me like that?"

The smile comes back, but it is sinister this time. It chills me more than anything else he's done.

"I still have your friends," he says. "And if you don't gather them soon, you will all be trapped down here. With me. *Forever.*"

He opens his mouth wide. Wider than his head. So wide it swallows up the sky. His teeth are fangs. Silver and sharp.

And then, with a terrifying roar, he swallows me whole.

Deshaun

I run through the dark, fleeing the wailing and scraping hands of the ghosts.

They are close. So close.

My heart hammers in my ears, and my lungs burn, and I can't see anything, nothing at all, and that is worse than seeing. That is the true horror of ghosts— you can never see what you're up against. You only know that they are there. Chasing you. Waiting to rip you apart. I'm never going to get out of here. This time, they won't vanish with the rising sun. They will trap me here.

Forever.

Giggling behind me, right by my ear.

I turn.

Catch the flash of blue eyes, razor-sharp teeth.

I trip.

And smash into a monster.

"Hey!" the monster yells.

No, not a monster.

"April?" I ask.

Her face is illuminated from the light of her cell phone.

"Deshaun!" I swear she blushes. "What—"

"We have to get out of here!" I interrupt. "The ghosts. We have to get away from them. We have to—"

"Deshaun, it's okay. I'm here. You were right. You were *right*. We have to face our fears. We have to. Otherwise we aren't getting out of here."

"You don't understand," I say. "I was wrong. I was so wrong. I tried to face my fears before and I just saw . . ."

I choke. I can't tell her what I saw. All of my friends in pain. All of them terrified. All because of me. Because I had been wrong.

"You weren't wrong," she says. She squeezes my shoulder. "*I* faced my fears, and I found you. We can do this, Deshaun. You just have to be brave."

Her hand falls from my shoulder and clasps my hand.

"You have to face them."

I nod.

And even though it's the last thing I want to do, I turn around and face the ghosts.

I don't see them. That's the worst part.

The light in April's hand goes out, and we are both plunged into darkness.

"It's okay," April says, her voice barely cutting through the gloom, even though she is walking right beside me. She squeezes. "We're okay. You're doing great."

We walk, and I hear them crying out. The ghosts.

Just like that night in the graveyard.

They cry out in pain, in agony. They yell my name. They tell me I will never escape. I will always be alone. Just like they are.

But I'm not alone.

I've never been alone.

It's the *ghosts* who have been alone this entire time. Not me. I've always had friends. I've always been loved.

I've always had a way out of the darkness.

April doesn't let go.

"You're doing it," she says.

And she's right. The howling grows weaker.

With every step, the light grows brighter.

Until the tunnel illuminates fully, and I see that we aren't in a graveyard at all. Just a long, twisting cave, with a light flickering at the end.

Distantly, I hear another wail. This one, I know, is human.

April hears it too.

"Caroline," she whispers, her eyes wide.

She doesn't let go of my hand; together, we run.

April

Deshaun and I rush into the cavern, nearly slamming into Andres and Kyle as they enter from another tunnel.

What we see is enough to make me consider turning around and running the other way.

The cavern is enormous and ringed with lanterns with guttering red and orange flames that cast terrifying shadows on the ceiling. Almost as terrifying as the clown, larger than life, standing on the far end in his shiny satin outfit, a shovel held in his dirty, gloved hands.

Almost as terrifying as the screams coming out of the open grave at his feet.

Caroline.

"It's too late for her," the clown jeers. "But not too late for you. I'll give you a choice. Leave her here with me, and I will let you go. You never liked her, anyway. She was mean to you. To all of you. You know your lives would be better off without her."

I look to the others.

The clown's words are harsh, but the worst part is knowing that they are all things I thought myself. But that was before. Before I knew why she was hurting. Before I knew what had made her so mean. A part of me worries that the others will agree with the clown. That they will turn around and leave me here to save the one girl I never thought I'd want or have to save.

Instead, they take a step forward. We all do.

"No," I say. "We aren't leaving without her."

The clown's face switches to anger, and then to glee, in the space of a heartbeat. His mouth curls into a venomous smile.

"Then you aren't leaving at all," he growls.

He drops the shovel.

"I will devour you. One. By. One."

He lifts a finger and points it
straight
at
me.

"And I will start with *you*."

The clown lunges.

Everyone sparks into action at once.

Kyle and Andres run to the side while Deshaun leaps in front of me. I barely have time to wonder if Kyle and Andres are leaving before the clown is on top of Deshaun, snarling and hissing like a feral dog. The clown's teeth are long and snakelike, its mouth so huge it's grotesque, and its gloved hands have turned into claws.

Deshaun cries out in fear and pain as he struggles against the clown. I leap to his aid, wrapping my arms around the clown's neck and trying to pry it off. It thrashes against me, trying to throw me.

"Let him go!" I yell. "It's me you want!"

The clown doesn't answer, just snarls loudly and tosses me to the side.

I grunt in pain, stars exploding across my vision as the breath leaves my lungs. I don't lie there, though.

I push myself up to standing, ignoring the pain in my side, and jump back toward the clown. I grab on to his arm as he pulls back to claw at Deshaun.

"Over here!" Andres calls. "April, bring him here!"

I glance over my shoulder, briefly, and see that the boys haven't run away after all. They stand by the grave, covered in dirt. And they have Caroline.

The grave.

That's it!

I yell out as I struggle with the clown, pulling him back and off of Deshaun. The boys are there in a heartbeat, each grabbing one of the clown's limbs.

The clown roars in anger, making the entire cave shake and the lights flicker.

Together, the three of us drag the clown back to the grave. Deshaun hobbles to his feet and stares at us, then comes to my side and grabs the clown's free leg, yanking him back.

It feels like it takes forever. It feels like we are fighting a bear.

The clown roars and yells, more animal than human, the entire cave shuddering with his rage.

A part of me knows I should be terrified. Knows that I should let go and run away and beg forgiveness because there is no way we could ever beat this creature, no way it will ever rest now that it knows us, now that it's found us.

Now that it's tasted our fear.

Then I look at my friends, the struggle on their faces, the sweat on their brows, and I know I will never give up. I will never turn back. Not now.

We reach the grave and manage to get him over the pit. I glance down quickly to see the open casket that Caroline had been trapped in. She stands at the side of the grave, watching us all with wide eyes and dirt smudging her pale cheeks. She is frozen in shock, still as a statue.

But the clown won't go in.

Its arms thrash wildly, and it's all we can do to hold on. Even as we struggle, its arms and legs seem to grow longer. Like spider legs. Clinging to the sides of the pit. Refusing to give in.

"We aren't going to make it!" Andres yells out. "It's too strong!"

"Your fear makes me stronger!" the clown yells gleefully.

Only . . . we aren't afraid.

We are determined.

So then . . .

Things click for me the same moment they do for her.

"Oh!" Caroline gasps. Her eyes light up with clarity.

Immediately, she leaps for the clown, wrapping her arms tight around its neck.

The clown roars in defeat. Dirt rains from the ceiling.

But it works.

Its arms and legs retract to a normal length. And, together, we manage to force it down into the grave. Caroline stays on its back, her arms around its neck and her legs around its torso. It continues to shrink, now only the size of her. Once it's down in the casket, she twists around and grabs for my outstretched hand. I lift her out, but the clown grabs after her. She kicks its hand and then kicks the casket shut.

The clown hammers its hands on the lid, howling. And I know that it will escape, that the latch won't hold. Caroline seems to gather this at the same time. She wrenches herself from my grasp and falls back on top of the lid.

"Do it!" she yells. "Bury it!"

"But what about you?" I yell.

"I'll be fine," she says back, her voice hitching over the sound of the wailing clown. "I have to face my fear too. And this is how I have to do it. Hurry!"

I look at the boys. Their eyes are wide. Disbelieving. We don't have time.

I grab the shovel and start pushing dirt into the grave. On top of the casket. And on top of Caroline.

The clown wails and Caroline keeps her eyes and mouth closed as we pile more and more dirt on top of them. Until we can't see the casket, even though it shakes the earth with its struggle.

Until we can't see Caroline.

Soon, all the dirt is back on the grave.

Caroline and the clown are buried.

"She's still in there," I say. I drop to my knees and clench my fingers into the soil. "Come on, Caroline. You can do it. You can make it. We're here for you!"

We all kneel there in silence. Staring at the grave. Waiting and hoping that Caroline will be able to escape.

She faced her fear of being buried.

She should be allowed to escape. Just like we did.

Moments turn to minutes. And soon, the silent cave no longer rumbles. The dirt doesn't move.

"Come on, Caroline," I whisper. A tear falls down my cheek, lands in the soil. "Please."

Deshaun puts his hand on my shoulder.

"I think she's gone, April," he says.

I shake my head. "No. She can't be. We have to save her. She saved us! We can't just leave her."

I start to dig with my hands. Andres comes over to help.

The dirt shifts in front of me.

I freeze.

Is it the clown, or Caroline?

And then, up from the dirt, shoots a tiny hand. Pale skin. And chipped, painted fingernails.

"Caroline!" I yell.

We all drop to our knees and dig.

We aren't leaving without all five of us. The clown had said it as a threat, but I will fulfill it as a promise.

Epilogue

Caroline

We sit together on the swing set down at the park, watching the other kids mill about. It's a beautiful, sunny afternoon, and that makes everyone want to stick around. To stay a little longer.

I look to my friends. My *real* friends. Deshaun and Andres and Kyle and April.

Deshaun pushes April on the swing, and she giggles like no one else is watching. Andres swings beside her; every once in a while, Kyle rushes up behind him and gives him a push, sending him laughing and flying high.

It's been a few weeks since we faced the clown.

None of us have had a nightmare since. None of us have seen anything bad or scary.

I don't think I've ever slept so well.

I don't think I've ever felt so happy. So *alive*.

My dad and I have even started talking about Mom. The things we loved, the things we remember. It's hard. But it brings us closer. And when we face the loss together, we remember we have each other.

I smile at my friends.

We faced the loss together. And we have each other.

Andres slows his swinging and looks over to Deshaun.

"If you ever need advice on how to deal with annoying brothers," Andres says, "I'm your guy. I have way too many."

Deshaun chuckles.

"Nah, it's fine. I've practically lived with Kyle my entire life. Having him *actually* move in to the guest room just means his dirty laundry is no longer on my bed."

"Hey!" Kyle says with a smile. "I don't leave dirty laundry. That was always you. I am very clean, thank you." He laughs. "If anything, I should be grateful that *your* stuff is no longer getting mixed up with *mine*."

Deshaun rolls his eyes.

"What should we do tonight?" April asks. "Scary movie at mine?"

I laugh. "Maybe not a scary movie. But I'm in."

"Us too," Andres and Kyle echo.

"Actually," Deshaun says, "why don't we do it at mine? We can have a little housewarming party for Kyle, now that he's officially part of the family."

"Yeah!" Andres says. "We can help you arrange your room."

Kyle chuckles. "I've seen your room. I think I'll have Caroline help me organize, thanks."

I don't remember the last time I had friends like this. Friends who supported one another, who didn't judge or bully. It feels like how friends should be.

"Come on," April says. "Let's go. We can grab some pizzas on the way."

"I want pepperoni!" Andres shouts, hopping off the swing. He takes Kyle's hand, and April comes over and takes mine, and Deshaun takes hers, and we all walk off the playground together, laughing and talking about what movies we will watch, and whether or not we should make popcorn.

We pass by the flagpole, and I notice two boys standing there, huddled together, looking at something.

"What do you think it means?" I hear one of them ask. I don't know their names. They must be fifth graders.

"I don't know," the other says. "Do you think we should do it?"

I glance at what they hold.

A piece of orange paper.

I can't read the writing, but I know the font. Despite the warmth of the sun and my friends, my heart goes cold.

"Why not?" I hear the first one say. "It's just the graveyard." He looks at me and lowers his voice before telling his friend: "There's nothing to be afraid of."

Acknowledgments

For a book about fear, this one has been an absolute blast to write, and I want to thank everyone who helped bring it about. First, my undying gratitude goes to Jana Haussmann, for sparking the idea and inspiring such a terrifying tale. Did she know that I grew up with life-size portraits of clowns in my living room (don't ask)? Probably not, but it seemed cosmic that we should work on this book together. And my deepest thanks go to my editor, David Levithan, for all of his keen insight—especially on how to add humor to something so scary (like sharks in the middle of Iowa! Though . . . I'm from Iowa, and I was totally afraid of sharks in the pool. And yes, that's another ellipsis for you to edit. Sorry not sorry!). My thanks as well to my agent, Brent Taylor, for rooting for me all the way.

I want to thank Scholastic and the Book Fairs for all of their amazing support—their enthusiasm for scary stories has been overwhelming, and I am so grateful to have such a wonderful team behind me. I couldn't have done any of this without you. A special shout-out as well to Nina Goffi for creating yet another terrifying cover. I can say without doubt that you will be giving all of us nightmares. And causing many passersby to wonder why I have a photo of a creepy clown as my phone background.

Finally, and most importantly, I want to thank you, the readers and teachers, for not only reading and sharing your love of scary stories, but for the fantastic letters and emails that brighten my day. Hearing from you truly means the world.

I hope my books will continue to scare and delight you for many years to come.

About the Author

K.R. Alexander is the pseudonym for author Alex R. Kahler.

As K.R., he writes creepy middle grade books for brave young readers. As Alex—his actual first name—he writes fantasy novels for adults and teens. In both cases, he loves writing fiction drawn from true life experiences. (But this book can't be real . . . can it?)

Alex has traveled the world collecting strange and fascinating tales, from the misty moors of Scotland to the humid jungles of Hawaii. He is always on the move, as he believes there is much more to life than what meets the eye.

You can learn more about his travels and books, including *The Collector, The Fear Zone,* and the books in the Scare Me series, on his website: cursedlibrary.com

He looks forward to scaring you again . . . soon.

Be afraid. Be very afraid.
K. R. Alexander's latest is
coming to haunt you.

1

"Ewww, I have fake blood on my shirt!"

I glance over to Julie, who—sure enough—has bright red corn syrup dripping down from the pocket of her T-shirt.

Tanesha breaks into laughter.

"That was me," she says. "I put a blood capsule in your pocket. Don't worry—it will wash out."

Julie glowers over at her, but Julie's anger never lasts very long. Almost immediately, she starts laughing.

"Good one, Tanesha, but just remember—"

"I don't get mad, I get even," both Tanesha and I say. And then we all start giggling. It's Julie's favorite phrase. But I'm pretty certain that she's never actually tried to get even.

Which is good, because Tanesha is a master prankster. If Julie tried to pull one over on her, I don't think it would end well.

Still giggling, we continue carrying our crates of scary props to the big old mansion in front of us. Three stories tall, with fading blue paint, huge windows, and a yard the size of a football field, Corvidon Manor is our town's largest and oldest home. Most of the year, it's a history museum, where people can look at old photographs of our town or talk to Mr. Evans, the proprietor, who gives free tours. I've been inside a few times for school field trips. From November to September, it's pretty boring.

Then October arrives.

For the month of October, Corvidon Manor is our playground. Every Halloween, Happy Hills holds a fund-raiser for our animal shelter. Four teams of kids each design a creepy experience for the mansion, one per floor, including the basement. The one with the scariest floor gets a year's supply of pizza and ice cream from Jolly Jerry's Pizzeria.

For the other teams, it's just a fun way to raise